Grace!

Flinging himself onto his back, he raked savage hands through his damp tumbled hair, feeling the familiar pangs of frustration knifing through his loins. He was hard and aroused by the emotions his unconscious mind had generated, his head still filled with images of her slim body spread-eagled beneath him, her hands cool and delicious against his hot flesh.

With a groan of disgust Oliver tore the cover aside and pushed himself up from the bed.

Dear Reader

I can't believe it, but this is my 150th book. Amazing! Once again, I must thank all my readers, old and new, who make writing such a pleasure. When I started, over thirty-five years ago, my daughter was a baby and my son hadn't even been born yet. Now they're grown with lives of their own—and I'm still writing.

My books have grown also. Times have changed and modern romances have to reflect the modern world, don't they?

Oliver, my hero in this story, has flaws, but he's also one of the most attractive men I've ever written about. Grace is beautiful—but she hasn't found it an advantage so far. It's hard for her to believe in her heart what she feels with her senses.

Well, read on and find out for yourself how both Oliver and Grace solve their differences. I hope you enjoy it. I certainly loved writing it.

Here's to the next—well, fifty, anyway!

Anne Mather

THE FORBIDDEN MISTRESS

BY
ANNE MATHER

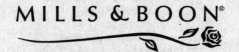

MILLS & BOON®

First published in Great Britain 2004
Harlequin Mills & Boon Limited,
Eton House, 18-24 Paradise Road, Richmond, Surrey TW9 1SR

© Anne Mather 2004

ISBN 0 263 83777 7

Set in Times Roman 10½ on 11½ pt.
01-1004-53733

Printed and bound in Spain
by Litografia Rosés, S.A., Barcelona

CHAPTER ONE

OLIVER was standing staring out of the long plate-glass windows of his fourteenth-storey office when the intercom on the desk behind him emitted a low buzz.

Sighing, he turned away from the view of the rain-wet Newcastle streets and strode across the wide expanse of dark blue broadloom to depress the button that connected him with his secretary next door. 'Yes?' he said shortly, not welcoming the interruption, and Mrs Clements cleared her throat before replying.

'It's your brother, Mr Ferreira,' she said, momentarily stunning him into silence. 'I told him you were busy, but he insists that you'll see him.' She paused. 'Will you?'

Oliver was still getting over the fact that his brother had had the nerve to come here when he heard the altercation in the outer office. Thomas Ferreira would resent being subjected to any delay and a moment later Oliver's door swung wide. A tall broad-shouldered man stood belligerently on the threshold with the diminutive figure of Mrs Clements hovering anxiously behind.

'What the hell is this?' he demanded, his fair good-looking features flushed with angry colour. 'Do I need an appointment to see you these days, Oliver? I know it's a while since we've spoken to one another, but for God's sake, lighten up, can't you?'

Oliver released the button of the intercom and straightened away from the broad slab of granite that topped his desk. Ignoring his brother, he looked beyond his stocky frame to the nervous figure of his secretary. 'It's all right,

Mrs Clements,' he said reassuringly. 'I know you did your best not to let him in.'

Mrs Clements clasped her hands together. 'You won't forget you've agreed to see Mr Adler at four o'clock, will you, Mr Ferreira?'

'He won't forget,' stated Thomas rudely, taking charge of the door. 'And I don't intend to keep him long, so don't look so worried. I'm only his brother, not the tax inspector.'

Mrs Clements ignored that comment and managed to wedge herself between the closing door and its frame. 'Is there anything I can get you, Mr Ferreira? Some tea or coffee, perhaps?'

'So long as it's not a bottle of Scotch,' Thomas interposed caustically, but Oliver disregarded the younger man and said politely, 'Some tea, Mrs Clements, if it's not too much trouble?'

'Of course it's not too much trouble.' Thomas mocked the woman's reply as he closed the door and rested for a moment against the mahogany panels. 'Honestly, Oliver, surely you know that woman would walk on hot coals, if you asked her.' He pulled a wry face. 'Most women would, for that matter.'

'But not all,' observed Oliver, feeling a momentary twinge of bitterness in his gut. Then, his dark eyes narrowing impatiently, 'What do you want, Tom? As you just heard, I don't have a lot of time.'

Tom's response was to leave the door and walk towards his brother's desk, pulling out one of the upright leather chairs used by visitors and lounging into it. 'Let's wait until the tea comes, shall we?' he suggested tightly. 'I'd prefer it if old Clements wasn't a party to what I have to say.'

Oliver suppressed his irritation. 'Mrs Clements is perfectly trustworthy,' he said. 'You don't have to worry that she'll gossip about anything she hears.'

'Even so...' Tom shrugged, looking about him. 'I'd forgotten what a view you have from this office,' he continued obliquely. 'I bet you missed it, too, when you were holed up at the Abbey.'

Oliver's nostrils flared and he was tempted to eject his brother from the office forthwith. But to do so would arouse more questions than answers and, until he'd heard whatever Tom had to say, he decided to contain his wrath.

But that didn't alter the way he felt about seeing him again. It had been almost four years since they'd had a serious conversation and, although he resented his gall in coming here, he couldn't deny a certain curiosity as to why his brother was here.

Yet, perhaps it was time that they put the past behind them. They'd been good friends when they were boys before Tom's treachery, and the collapse of Oliver's marriage, had driven them apart. The fact that it had been as much Sophie's fault as his brother's that the marriage had broken down was something he'd had to live with. After all, she had been his wife, while Tom had been a free man.

Of course, that still didn't alter the fact that he would find it hard to trust his brother again. Oliver's divorce from Sophie had been painful and destructive and for months the only respite he'd found was at the bottom of a glass. Tom's snide comments about the bottle of Scotch and his reference to Oliver's stay at Blackstone Abbey—a well-known centre for those needing an escape from either drugs or alcohol—were evidence that his brother wasn't here to make amends for his behaviour. He probably wanted something, thought Oliver bitterly. That was usually why he'd come to him in the past.

Subsiding into his own chair behind the desk, Oliver leaned back and steepled his fingers, regarding the other man speculatively. Tom looked older, he decided without prejudice. But then, so did he. Trauma—particularly emotional trauma—did that to you.

'How's Sophie?' he asked at last, deciding to get it over with, and was surprised at how little emotion he felt. For months after the divorce, even hearing her name could arouse the destructive desire for oblivion. But now he felt only a trace of regret for what might have been, a rueful reminder of the gullible fool he used to be.

Tom looked surprised at the question. 'She's okay, I guess,' he answered offhandedly. 'Why don't you ring her and find out?'

It took an effort but Oliver managed not to look as stunned as he felt. 'I think not,' he said, his hands falling away to the arms of his chair as he sat forward. Then, as Mrs Clements reappeared with a tray he managed to summon a smile for her benefit. 'Thank you.' He viewed the plate of biscuits with feigned enthusiasm. 'This looks good.'

'If you need anything else, just let me know,' the older woman declared warmly. Her eyes flicked briefly over his visitor, and Oliver could practically tell what she was thinking. Mrs Clements was intensely loyal and she had been shocked and angered by his brother's betrayal.

'We will,' Tom answered now, deliberately bringing a flush of pink to her cheeks. He, too, had to be aware of the woman's feelings and it was his way of reminding her that her opinion meant less than nothing to him.

The door closed behind her, but Oliver made no attempt to touch the tea tray. If Tom wanted tea, he could help himself, he thought, once again leaning back in his chair. 'What do you want?' he asked, with a resigned sigh. 'If it's money, you're wasting your time. Apart from the fact that my ex-wife did her best to clean me out, there's been a downturn in the housing market.'

'Don't pretend your business relies on domestic contracts,' retorted Tom with some energy. 'I happen to know you've just made a deal to design the shopping complex they're going to build at Vicker's Wharf.' He scowled, his fair features losing much of their attraction. 'In any case, I haven't said I want money, have I? Since Sophie invested most of her divorce settlement in the garden centre, it's going from strength to strength.' He paused, as if reluctant to continue, but eventually he went on. 'As a matter of fact, I've just bought the smallholding that adjoins the centre and I'm hoping we can sell conservatories, too, in the future. They're the accessory of choice these days, as you probably know.'

'Good for you.'

Oliver was glad to hear his brother's business acumen was paying off. He had no problem in applauding his success. The Ferreira garden centre had been their father's business before his retirement, but Tom had been the only one of his sons to share his love of the soil. Since Tom had taken over the centre, the interest in gardening generally had enabled him to practically double the profits. That and Oliver's ex-wife's contribution, of course.

'Don't patronise me,' muttered his brother now, evidently hearing something other than simple approval in Oliver's voice. 'We can't all be academic geniuses. Some of us have fairly modest ambitions.'

Oliver refrained from arguing with him. This was an old grievance and one he had no wish to revisit. Tom knew full well that he was no genius, nor was he particularly academic. But he'd been good at maths at school and working with computers had been an automatic progression. The fact that his degree in computer science led to a career in design engineering had been just as natural to him as working in horticulture had been to his brother.

'So,' he said at last. 'If it's not money, what do you want? I can't believe you've come here to enquire after my health.'

'Why not?' Tom's response was swift and resentful.

'You're still my brother, aren't you? Just because we've had our differences in the past—'

'Seducing my wife and breaking up my marriage cannot be dismissed as "differences",' retorted Oliver curtly.

'I know, I know.' Tom looked sulky now. 'Like I say, we've had our problems. I'm not denying it. And I'm not denying that I was to blame.' He sniffed. 'But, dammit, I couldn't have seduced Sophie if she hadn't been willing, could I? You were always hell-bent on becoming a partner in Faulkner's. You neglected your wife, Oliver. Admit it.'

Oliver's jaw clamped. 'I have no intention of admitting anything to you, Tom. And if this is your way of justifying what you did—'

'It's not.' Tom interrupted him quickly, leaning forward in his chair, his expression rueful now, appealing. 'Look, would it make you feel any better if I told you that—that what happened was a mistake? It should never have gone as far as it did.' He chewed on his lower lip. 'I was a fool, a selfish, arrogant fool. You can't regret it any more than I do.'

Oliver's chair slammed back against the wall behind him as he got to his feet. 'I think you'd better go,' he said, the muscles in his jaw jerking furiously. Then he gave a short, mirthless laugh and shook his head disbelievingly. 'You really are priceless, do you know that? You actually thought that coming here and telling me you'd made a mistake—made a mistake, of all things—would be some consolation to me!'

Tom's chin jutted. 'I thought it might be,' he muttered peevishly. 'We all make mistakes, don't we?'

Oliver shook his head again. 'Just go, Tom. Before we both say something we'll regret.'

Tom hunched his shoulders then, but he didn't move, and Oliver glanced down wearily at the narrow watch on his wrist. It was half past three, he saw, half incredulously. Had it only been fifteen minutes since Tom appeared?

He blew out an impatient breath, regarding his brother's hunched figure with some ambivalence. What now? he wondered. Was the other man going to make him throw him out? He could, if he wanted to, he knew that. Although Tom was broad and bulky, Oliver was fitter and had at least four inches over him in height.

Yet he baulked at the prospect. The idea of propelling his brother through Mrs Clements' office and along the corridor that was flanked by other offices on either side was not something he relished. It had been hard enough suffering his colleagues' sympathy when Sophie left him and his subsequent dependence on alcohol that had ended with his sojourn at Blackstone Abbey. He had no wish to revive those memories, or give anyone the impression that he still cared enough to want to do his brother some harm. He didn't, he realised incredulously. All he felt was contempt that Tom should imagine he was fool enough to believe his lies.

'Look, I've got an appointment shortly,' he said, realising that getting angry wasn't going to do him any good. For some reason, Tom was determined to stick it out until he'd said what he wanted to say. And Oliver had the uneasy suspicion that the worst was yet to come.

'I know,' said Tom now. 'I heard what old Clements said.'

'Then you'll realise that you can't stay here,' declared Oliver crisply. 'I suggest you go before you make a complete ass of yourself.'

Tom looked up at him with accusing eyes. 'You don't care about me at all, do you? You don't care what happens to me?'

'What happens to *you*?' Oliver stared at him. 'Is that

what this is all about? You expect me to somehow put things right between us?'

Tom gave a shrug. 'Not exactly.'

'I'm pleased to hear it.'

Tom scowled. 'You're so smug. Why did I never realise it before? You don't care about anybody, do you, Oliver? God, no wonder Sophie was desperate for affection. She never got it from a cold bastard like you!'

Oliver was around the desk, with his hand fisted in a handful of the other man's shirt, hauling him up out of the chair before he could stop himself. 'You—misbegotten sonofabitch,' he growled, his fist drawing back to deliver the punch his brother so rightfully deserved. But when, instead of trying to defend himself, Tom merely closed his eyes and prepared to take his punishment, Oliver found he couldn't do it. With a stifled oath, he flung him back again and strode across to the windows, struggling to regain his composure.

There was silence in the room for several minutes after that. Oliver took the time to regulate his breathing, raking his fingers across his scalp, rumpling the thick mass of dark hair that brushed his collar at the back. He straightened the jacket of his light grey suit, checked that his tie fell smoothly against the pearl buttons of his white shirt. And did his best to remember that he was the victim here, not the apparently humbled man who still sat, unspeaking, in his chair.

Finally, he was forced to turn round again. It was almost twenty minutes to four and he had to get Tom out of there before Sidney Adler arrived. Adler was a local politician who had been instrumental in Faulkner's being given the contract to design the new shopping complex. He was also a close friend of Oliver's partner, Andrew Faulkner, and unlikely to be impressed by Oliver bringing his personal problems into the office.

Expelling another heavy sigh, he walked back to his desk and stood for a few moments looking down on Tom's bent head. Then he said wearily, 'What do you want, Tom? I can't give you absolution. And I doubt if Sophie will appreciate hearing that you've been here, talking to me.'

'She won't care,' said Tom, pulling a handkerchief out of his pocket and making a great play of blowing his nose. 'I've probably beaten her to it, actually. She wanted out of our relationship just as much as me.'

Oliver's jaw almost dropped. 'What?' he exclaimed disbelievingly. 'Did you come here to tell me you and Sophie have split up?'

'What else?' muttered Tom, with an indifferent gesture. 'At present, she's staying with her mother. Like I said before, it was all a terrible mistake.'

It was almost six o'clock when Oliver left the office.

Adler, he'd found, behaved like an old woman, and he'd spent at least half the time they were together gossiping about other local bureaucrats. There'd been little discussion of a useful nature and Oliver suspected he shouldn't have shown the old man the bottle of Scotch he kept for visitors. Adler had accepted more than one glass to lubricate his ramblings, and Oliver felt significantly hyper now with the amount of Diet Coke he'd had to consume for courtesy's sake.

His car was parked in the basement garage. A twelve-year-old Porsche, it had been Oliver's gift to himself when he'd first gone to work for Faulkner Engineering. It had also been the only luxury he'd refused to sell when Sophie left him. The house they'd shared had gone and most of his possessions. A necessity, in any case, as the loft apartment he'd moved into just didn't have room for most of them.

Before the divorce, he and Sophie had lived in an exclusive housing development north of Newcastle. It hadn't been far from the garden centre, which was also situated in a village north of the city, and they had seen quite a lot of his parents and brother then. However, since his father's retirement, his parents spent at least half the year abroad. They'd bought a villa in southern Spain, where his father's ancestors had originated, and the old man always boasted he was returning to his roots.

Now, reminiscing about his parents inevitably brought Oliver's thoughts back to his brother. It hadn't been easy persuading him to leave quietly, and even now Oliver wasn't entirely clear what his visit had been about. What had Tom anticipated? he wondered. That he'd be so delighted that Tom and Sophie had parted, all would be forgiven? It was the most naïve kind of reasoning and Tom wasn't that stupid.

So why had he come? What motive had he had for making the trip? Oliver doubted they could ever be friends again. Not after all that had happened. And if Tom was expecting a different reaction, he was going to be disappointed.

It briefly crossed his mind that Sophie might have sent him. If they'd separated, as he'd said, perhaps she had some idea of resurrecting their relationship. Which was equally ludicrous. Besides, he was flattering himself if he imagined she was hedging her bets.

In any case, he had no desire to rekindle his relationship with his ex-wife. Whatever she thought, whatever interpretation she'd put on the emotional trauma he'd suffered when she left him, he was over it now. And it had never been wholly about Sophie. His brother's betrayal had meant equally much, he realised now.

Nevertheless, he'd had to agree to see Tom again. It had been the only way to get him out of the office before Adler turned up. Considering Adler's penchant for gossip, Oliver had had no desire to learn that he'd provided juicy fodder at the next party conference.

They'd agreed to meet the following lunchtime at The Crown in Tayford. It was years since Oliver had visited the pub, which was just a short distance from his parents' home. Fortunately, his mother and father were away at the moment so there'd be no question of them getting involved. He knew his mother worried about his estrangement from his brother, and she was bound to think they were healing their differences if she knew.

On impulse, Oliver turned in the opposite direction to his quayside apartment. A desire to see the garden centre again had him driving north out of Newcastle, heading towards the airport. But before then, he turned west towards Belsay on the road that delved deep into the Northumbrian countryside.

Although Oliver had been born in the area, it was some years since he'd enjoyed making this journey. But with the rain giving way to the watery sunshine of a May evening, he felt an unaccustomed sense of well-being.

Before reaching Belsay, he turned left yet again onto a narrow country road with high hedges on either side. The garden centre had been signposted from the major road and it was only about a quarter of a mile farther on, on the outskirts of Ridsgate, the nearest village to Tayford itself.

Ferreira's Plant World looked an impressive place viewed from the road. It had built up a fair reputation in recent years and people came quite a distance to wander round its gardens and greenhouses. As well as the usual ranks of hothouses, there were a shop, a café, a florist and a play area for children. And, although it was already after six o'clock, it was still doing a thriving business.

There were several cars in the parking area and, although he hadn't intended to stop, Oliver found himself easing the Porsche into a convenient space. He sat for a few minutes, drumming his thumbs on the steering wheel, wondering what the hell he was doing here. And then, deciding he couldn't leave without satisfying himself that Tom really wasn't in financial difficulties, he switched off the engine and got out of the car.

He saw her as he was locking the Porsche. She was standing near one of the greenhouses, apparently supervising the loading of sacks of compost onto a flatbed utility truck that she obviously intended to drive to another part of the site.

She was tall, easily five feet nine, and he told himself it was her height that had attracted his attention. But with long legs encased in the tightest jeans he'd ever seen and a trim yet shapely body, she was instantly noticeable. And that without taking into account her warm, luminous beauty and a mane of red-gold hair, secured in a single fat braid that had an impact all its own.

Perhaps it was the intentness of his stare that made her aware he was watching her. Eyes fringed by long, dark eyelashes turned in his direction and for a moment a quizzical expression crossed her face. Then one of the two men loading the truck spoke to her and she looked away, but not before a faint smile of inquiry—invitation?—touched her generous mouth.

Deciding he was definitely letting his imagination run away with him, Oliver pocketed his keys and strolled towards the gardens. By avoiding the shop, he was hoping to avoid being recognised by the older members of Tom's staff.

There was no sign of Tom, however, and he couldn't decide if he was glad or sorry. Now he'd have no excuse for not keeping their appointment tomorrow. At the bottom of him he supposed he'd hoped he could find out what was going on without wasting a couple of hours in futile discussion.

He walked to the far end of the site, noticing that his brother had been as good as his word. Already work had started on digging up the land immediately adjoining the garden centre. An excavator was residing amid a clutter of other machinery, and in the distance what used to be the home of the previous owner was being levelled to the ground.

'It looks pretty ugly, doesn't it?' remarked a husky voice behind him. Oliver turned quickly to find the girl he had seen earlier relaxing against one of a pair of stone sundials abandoned beside the fence. Closer now, Oliver could see that her skin was creamy soft, like a peach, her nose straight and not too prominent, wide eyes an incredible shade of green.

Gathering his wits, he said, 'I guess it does.' He pushed his hands into his jacket pockets and tried to dilute his gaze. 'But all building projects are like that in the early stages.'

'And you'd know,' she said, surprising him. 'You're a design engineer.' And at his raised eyebrows, she added easily, 'You're Tom's brother, Oliver, I think. He said he might be seeing you today.'

Oliver sucked in his breath. 'Did he?'

'Yes. He didn't say you were coming here, though.' She smiled, revealing a row of even white teeth. 'I'm Grace Lovell, by the way. I know he'll be pleased to see you,' she went on, returning to her earlier theme. 'Mrs Ferreira said you've been estranged for some time.'

'Mrs Ferreira?' Oliver frowned. He hadn't realised Sophie was still calling herself by that name.

'Your mother,' explained Grace, apparently sensing his confusion. 'I know your parents quite well. They spend a lot of time in San Luis.'

Oliver revised his original opinion. 'You're Spanish?' he asked incredulously, but she shook her head.

'Not at all, I'm afraid. My father's an American, actually.

But he works for the British government, so I've spent most of my life in England.'

'I see.' Oliver paused. 'And the San Luis connection?'

'My parents own a villa in San Luis, too. That's where I met Tom, actually. And how I persuaded him to give me this job.'

Oliver absorbed this. 'And do you like it? The job, I mean?'

She shrugged, straightening away from the sundial, and he was once again struck by her height. But unlike a model, she was built on more generous lines, and, despite the fact that she didn't appear to be wearing a bra, her breasts were firm and high—

And where the hell had that come from? he wondered, arresting himself instantly. He was getting far too interested in her altogether. Dammit, it was years since he'd noticed a strange woman's breasts. It was no excuse that the cold air had made them more noticeable. She was probably frozen, he decided, aware of the hard peaks against her thin tee shirt. It was also obvious that the heat he was feeling was definitely not climate-induced.

'It's okay,' she said, and it took him a minute to realise she was answering his question and not excusing his too-personal appraisal. 'I thought I wanted to teach when I left college, but after six years working in an inner-city comprehensive I decided I needed a change of scene.'

Oliver made a gesture of assent and they started back towards the main building, Grace falling into step beside him with a lithe, easy stride. As he walked he realised he had to revise his estimate of how old she was as well. He'd guessed twenty-two or twenty-three, but now thirty didn't seem so far off the mark.

Not that it mattered. Just because she was older than he'd imagined didn't change his own position at all. He, after all, was thirty-four, with a history no one would envy and a current girlfriend. Besides, she probably had a boyfriend. She was far too attractive to remain unattached for long.

'Have you been here long?' he asked now, wishing he had an excuse not to go into the shop. He hadn't corrected her when she'd assumed he hadn't seen his brother yet, and it was going to be bloody awkward if Tom turned up.

'Seven months, give or take,' she said. She grimaced. 'All through one of the worst winters on record! Two of the greenhouses were flooded. We had to come to work in wellington boots!'

Oliver managed a faint smile. 'A baptism of fire.'

'Well, of water,' she remarked humorously. Then she laughed. 'What an idiot! Baptisms are usually in water, aren't they?'

Oliver grinned, and he was just about to ask her what she thought about the north of England when her face changed. Her cheeks turned a little pink and he thought at first how charmingly unaffected she was. But then another female voice spoke his name and he stifled a groan as he turned to acknowledge his ex-wife.

CHAPTER TWO

SOPHIE—Sherwood now, he assumed—was striding towards them from the direction of the car park. 'Oliver,' she said warmly, before her gaze shifted to his companion, dismissing her. 'I thought I recognised the car. Oh, Oliver, it's so good to see you.'

It was the last thing he'd expected her to say. And the most incredible. They'd hardly parted on friendly terms. Oliver had been disgusted by the fact that her affair with Tom had been going on for months before he'd learned of it. And Sophie herself had been eager to blame him, to accuse him of neglecting her and thinking more of his rotten business than he did of his wife.

To meet her now, to have her announce it was good to see him again, was ludicrous. He'd hoped never to have to meet her again. He wouldn't have come here today if he'd suspected his ex-wife might be on the premises.

With a sideways glance at the young woman beside him, he realised he couldn't speak freely in front of her. Instead, suppressing his irritation, he inclined his head. 'Sophie,' he greeted her noncommittally. Then, because he couldn't think of anything else to add that wouldn't be construed as contentious, 'I didn't know you worked here.'

'I don't.' Sophie's scornful denial was revealing. 'But your brother owes me some money. Did he tell you?' She cast another look at Grace. 'What are you waiting for? I'd like to speak to my husband in private.'

Husband? Oliver winced, but Grace seemed unperturbed by Sophie's implied rebuke. Turning to Oliver, she said, 'Perhaps I'll see you later. Tom shouldn't be long.'

20

'If he can drag himself out of the pub, you mean?' remarked Sophie coldly. 'I wouldn't hold your breath.'

'Tom's not at the pub,' Grace retorted evenly. 'He had an appointment at the bank, as you probably know. Besides, he won't be long when he knows his brother is waiting for him.'

But Tom didn't even know he was there, Oliver reflected, though he was unwilling to admit it. He didn't want to say anything to give his ex-wife more ammunition. He didn't know what was going on here, but it was obvious Sophie didn't like the younger woman. Why? Was she jealous of her? He decided he'd prefer not to pursue that thought to its obvious conclusion.

'Whatever,' Sophie said, now moving forward and slipping her arm though his. And, although he carefully detached himself, she insisted on staying close to his side as she edged him towards the pools that exhibited tropical fish. 'That's better,' she murmured with satisfaction as a glance over his shoulder saw Grace look after them for a moment and then walk away in the opposite direction. Her tone grew suddenly venomous. 'I don't know how that woman has the nerve to speak to me!'

'Why? Don't you like her?' Oliver halted abruptly, refusing to go any further without an explanation. 'What's going on, Sophie? What has Grace done to you? And why the sudden urge for my company? I know you and Tom have split up so, please, don't pretend it has anything to do with me.'

Sophie stared at him. 'You've seen Tom?'

'This afternoon.' Oliver's tone was flat.

'Then he must have told you about Grace.'

'Told me what?' But Oliver suspected he already knew. Sophie wasn't particularly subtle when it came to personal matters.

She sniffed and shook her head, looking at him appealingly. 'You don't know what it's been like for me,' she exclaimed. 'Since that woman came to work at the garden centre, things have gone from bad to worse.'

Oliver looked about him critically. 'I'd have said the place was thriving,' he remarked, and she uttered a most unladylike expletive.

'In our relationship,' she corrected him tersely. 'Tom and I were already having problems before she came along. I'll admit it. But I never dreamed he'd already found my replacement.'

Oliver felt a depressingly familiar sense of *déjà vu*. Not that he'd been seriously considering getting involved with someone who worked for his brother, he assured himself, but the news that Grace Lovell was Tom's latest conquest wasn't what he wanted to hear. She was too good for his brother, he thought grimly. Tom had already wrecked his marriage. He wouldn't like to see him wreck her life as well.

He should have known, he grumbled silently. When Tom came to see him that afternoon, he should have guessed there was someone else involved. From the age of puberty, Tom had slept with countless women. He'd never married any of them, of course. Not even Sophie. So why should he, Oliver, have imagined that their relationship was any different?

'He met her in Spain last year,' Sophie was going on now, evidently under the mistaken impression that Oliver might be interested. 'He's gone out there before, when I've been unable to go with him. Not that your mother and father really want to see me, in any case. I'm *persona non grata* where they're concerned.'

'Sophie—'

'He used to make the excuse that he needed to talk business with your father,' she went on seamlessly. 'I had no reason to doubt him. He and George often have their heads together when your father's at home. I admit, he did seem a bit detached this time when he got home, but I put it down to his health. He'd said he was feeling a bit under the weather before he went away.'

Oliver held up both hands now, palms out to silence her. 'Is this going somewhere, Sophie?' he asked. 'Because if not, I've got other things to do.'

Sophie's eyes filled with tears. 'Don't be unkind to me, Oliver. I couldn't bear it if you abandoned me. I know I've behaved abominably in the past, but you have to believe I regret it now.'

'Sophie—'

'No, listen to me. Perhaps it's partly my fault that Tom found someone else. I kept comparing him to you. Yes, I did.' This as Oliver gave her an incredulous stare. 'It's true. Tom and I were never meant to be together. I don't know why I ever listened to his lies.'

'That's it. I'm out of here.'

Oliver had heard enough. Any minute now, she was going to say that she'd never stopped loving him and that she hoped he'd take her back.

As if.

Oliver scowled. When he'd had the—what he now acknowledged was a crazy—notion to make this diversion, he'd had no idea he'd be opening this can of worms. He'd wanted to see the garden centre. He'd half hoped he'd encounter his brother and get it over with. Now he didn't know what to think. What did Tom really want from him?

Sophie had burst into tears at his words, her pale, delicate features stark and drawn. She'd aged, too, Oliver mused, resisting the comparison to Grace Lovell. But he knew his ex-wife well enough to realise that most of her distress was just an act.

'Don't go like this, Oliver,' she begged now. 'Please. You've got to help me. Tom says he can't give me back the money I invested in the business, and I can't support myself on what I earn at the charity shop.'

The money she'd invested in the business was her divorce settlement, but Oliver didn't remind her of that. 'Get another job,' he said carelessly, heading towards the car park. He'd had enough of other people's problems for one day.

'I can't,' said Sophie desperately, trailing after him. 'I don't have any qualifications. You surely wouldn't like to see your wife working behind the tills in some supermarket?'

'Why not? Other women do it.' Oliver paused when he reached his car. 'And you're not my wife, Sophie,' he added, and for the first time it felt good to say it. 'I'm sorry if things haven't worked out the way you wanted, but that's life. Get over it.'

Sophie's chin wobbled, a tactic that would have tugged at his conscience years ago. But no longer. With a brief, 'Tell Tom I couldn't wait,' he coiled his length behind the steering wheel, aware that he burned rubber as he accelerated out of the car park.

Grace saw Oliver leave from the window of the coffee shop. The small café was closing and she was helping Lucy Cameron clear the tables so the older woman could get away on time. Lucy had a family, four kids, all of school age, and Grace knew she didn't like them being alone in the house after dark.

'Was that who I think it was?' Lucy asked now, joining Grace at the window as the Porsche peeled away off the site.

'Who did you think it was?' asked Grace, reluctant to sound too knowledgeable, and Lucy stepped back to give the younger woman a considering stare.

'Well, it looked like Tom's brother,' she said. 'I'd know

that old Porsche he drives anywhere. I don't know why he doesn't get himself a new car. It's not as if he couldn't afford it.'

Grace eased her hands into the front pockets of her jeans. 'Do you know him well?' she asked, careful not to sound too interested, and Lucy shrugged before returning to her job of stacking the dishwasher.

'Fairly well,' she replied now. 'Though it's some time since I've seen him around here.' She paused. 'Did I see you talking to him? Didn't he tell you who he was?'

Grace coloured, turning away so that Lucy couldn't see her face. 'I recognised him,' she said. 'He looks a bit like Tom, don't you think? He's darker, of course. And taller. But their features aren't dissimilar.'

Lucy gave her a wry look. 'It sounds to me as if you gave him a thorough once-over,' she remarked. She frowned. 'I always liked Oliver. I was really sorry when he and his brother fell out over—'

But she didn't finish her sentence, and Grace guessed at once why she'd suddenly acquired an unexpected interest in the contents of the till. The clatter of heels on the tiled floor had warned her that they were no longer alone, and she was hardly surprised when Sophie Ferreira came purposefully towards her.

'Where's Tom?' Sophie fairly spat the words, her bristling personality making up for what she lacked in height. 'You can tell me now. I realise you were trying to protect him from Oliver, but he's gone.'

'I know.' Despite the fact that she knew what Sophie thought of her, Grace refused to be intimidated. She had nothing to be ashamed of. She and Tom were friends, nothing more. 'And I don't know where Tom is. Perhaps he is at the pub. Why don't you go and find out?'

'Don't you dare tell me what to do.' Sophie's angry response was out of all proportion to the offence. Clearly something hadn't suited her and Grace was being made the scapegoat. 'Anyway, when he does come back, tell him I want to see him. I'll wait at the house. I've still got my key.'

Grace shrugged. 'Okay.' But she knew Tom wouldn't like it. She didn't like it much herself. The possibility that Sophie might take the opportunity to check out where Grace was sleeping now that she'd left had her hands balling into fists. But there was nothing she could do about it.

'Right.'

If Sophie had expected an argument, she didn't get one, and after a brief assessing glance in Lucy's direction she turned and left the café. The two women saw her cross the yard to the car park and pull open the door of a late-model BMW. Then, following Oliver's example, she drove out of the yard, turning in the opposite direction from the one he had taken.

'Bitch,' said Lucy succinctly, passing Grace on her way to the door to turn the sign to 'Closed'. 'That woman is a grade one bitch! I don't know what Oliver ever saw in her.'

'Or Tom,' murmured Grace, but Lucy only grimaced.

'Tom deserved her,' she muttered, stomping back to the till. 'I hope Oliver realises how lucky he's been.'

Grace didn't feel qualified to answer her. Sophie's and Oliver's divorce had been final long before she came on the scene. She'd heard the gossip, of course. How Tom had had an affair with his brother's wife. But she'd also heard, from Tom admittedly, that Oliver had neglected Sophie in favour of his work. And no one could deny Sophie's part in the breakup. Once again, according to Tom, it had been Sophie who had encouraged him, not the other way about.

Grace decided it was not something she wanted to get into a discussion over. Her own position, as a paying guest in Tom's house, was open to enough speculation as it was. But when she'd come to work at the garden centre, Sophie and Tom had been living together. It had seemed a logical solution to her accommodation problem to accept Tom's offer of the spare room.

Now, however, things were different. Sophie and Tom had split up and Grace didn't know how to get out of staying in the house. The trouble was, it was so handy for the centre. On the outskirts of Tayford, not far from his parents' home.

Mr and Mrs Ferreira had been instrumental in her accepting Tom's offer in the first place. Grace wondered now if they'd had some intimation that all was not going well with their son and his lady friend—who just happened to be their other son's ex-wife—and had hoped her presence might act as a calming influence. If so, it hadn't worked. Sophie had never liked her, and Tom had attempted to compensate for her rudeness.

The upshot was, Sophie had got jealous and had started accusing her of having designs on Tom herself. Grace shook her head as she left Lucy to lock up the café and made her way to the offices that adjoined the main building. She liked Tom. Who wouldn't? He was easy to get along with. But he'd never given her that hot, melting feeling in the pit of her stomach that she'd experienced when she'd encountered Oliver Ferreira's dark gaze.

Just for a moment she wondered how she'd feel if she were sharing a house with Oliver. His lean, dark-skinned face and tall athletic body were so different from his brother's bland good looks. Oliver wasn't good-looking in the formal sense, but he was very attractive. And sexy, she conceded tensely. No wonder Sophie wanted him back.

And she did want him back, Grace would bet her life on it. There'd been so much pent-up aggression in her tone when she'd told Grace to get lost. Oh, not in so many words, of course, but Grace knew her well enough now to know what she was thinking. Sophie needed a man to lean on, and Tom hadn't come up to scratch.

She shivered then, wrapping her arms about herself and rubbing the bare flesh below the tight sleeves of her tee shirt. But it wasn't the cold that was making her antsy. The shiver she'd felt was purely anticipation. Despite what Sophie wanted her to think, she hoped she saw Oliver again.

She wasn't sure how she felt when she discovered Tom was in his office, working at the computer. He must have known Sophie was on the premises, and deliberately kept out of her way. If so, he'd missed seeing Oliver as well. Or was that deliberate, too?

He looked round with a smile when he saw who it was in the doorway. 'Hi,' he said, subjecting her to a far too familiar appraisal. 'How are things?'

'Things are okay, I guess,' said Grace slowly, propping her shoulder against the jamb. 'Sophie's at the house. Did you know?'

'Sophie?' He tried to sound surprised, but to her ears he failed abysmally. Then, as if realising he couldn't fool her, his mouth pulled down at the corners. 'I knew she was here,' he confessed with a grimace. 'I suppose she's still agitating on about her money?'

'I wouldn't know.' Grace refused to get involved in the ongoing saga. 'Anyway, I just thought I'd warn you. In case you'd just got back.' She sniffed the air. 'Have you been drinking? Sophie told Oliver you'd be at the pub, but I defended you.'

'Oliver!' Tom looked genuinely taken aback now. 'Oliver was here?'

'As you'd know for yourself, if you didn't spend so much time hiding from your girlfriend,' retorted Grace with feeling. 'Anyway, I'm leaving. I'm meeting a friend for a drink and I don't want to be late.'

Tom frowned. 'What friend?' he asked, and she was tempted to tell him to mind his own business. But she didn't.

'A friend from the gym,' she said. She spent a lot of her spare time at the leisure centre in Ponteland. Initially, she'd joined to give Tom and Sophie some time on their own. But lately, she'd been glad of a reason to avoid spending whole evenings alone with Tom. 'You don't know her,' she added, straightening. 'I'll get something to eat while I'm out.'

'Hey.' Tom got up from his chair. 'You still haven't told me what Oliver was doing here. Did he want to see me?' Then he grimaced impatiently. 'Of course, he must have done. Why else would he come here?'

'You tell me.' Grace would prefer not to discuss Oliver right now. 'Anyway, Sophie collared him as soon as she saw him.'

'Sophie?' Tom scowled now. 'Goddammit, why didn't you say so? She would have to turn up here today.'

'Does it matter?' Grace didn't understand his agitation. 'You said you were seeing him today. I assumed you must have arranged for him to visit.'

'Well, I didn't. I went to his office this afternoon, as a matter of fact.' Tom glanced at his watch now, and Grace decided it was time to beat a tactical retreat.

'I'll see you in the morning,' she said, deciding she would go to the cinema after her date with Cindy. The last thing she wanted was for Tom to have another row with Sophie and then expect her to provide a shoulder to cry on. 'Don't wait up.'

Tom swore. 'Do you have to meet this woman tonight?' he demanded irritably. 'After the day I've had, I could do without an undiluted diet of Sophie's complaints. Come on, Grace, you know what she's like. This will be another attempt to get her money. And I can't stand knowing she can sink this business if she chooses.'

Grace sighed. 'Surely things aren't that bad?'

'They're that bad,' Tom insisted. 'I wish I'd never encouraged her to invest in the first place.'

'But you did.' Grace frowned as a thought occurred to her. 'Was that why you wanted to see Oliver today? Surely you don't expect him to bail you out?'

'No!' Tom's tone was sharp. Then, as if realising there was no point in lying to her, he lifted his shoulders in defeat. 'Well, okay,' he conceded. 'Maybe I did entertain the thought that he might help me. He's family, isn't he? And it's not as if he couldn't afford it.'

Grace gaped at him. 'You can't be serious, Tom. Oliver has every reason to hate your guts!'

'Why? Because I took that hag away from him?' Tom snorted. 'He should be thanking me. He doesn't know when he's well off.'

'I don't think Oliver will see it that way,' said Grace honestly. Despite his initial interest in her, he'd abandoned her soon enough when his ex-wife had turned up. And it was obvious Sophie had her sights set on rekindling that relationship. The way she'd gushed all over Oliver had made Grace feel physically sick.

'He will,' said Tom confidently. 'I know Oliver. This was his father's business, too, remember? He won't want it to close. Just think how many people would be out of work.'

Grace conceded he might have a point. 'So why don't you ask your father for help?' she asked curiously. George Ferreira couldn't wait to get back to the garden centre when he came home.

'Dad doesn't have that kind of money,' Tom protested. 'Sophie put two hundred thousand into the business. How do you think I was able to buy the smallholding next door?'

Grace pulled a face. 'And you think Oliver will cover her investment?' she exclaimed incredulously. 'Tom, that's a pipedream and you know it.'

His scowl reappeared and he strode restlessly about the office. 'He's got to,' he muttered. 'It's a good investment.'

'And did you tell him this?' asked Grace. 'Were you up front with him? Is that why he came here today, to check out how we're doing?'

'No, no and no,' muttered Tom, hunching his shoulders. 'I didn't get around to it. He threatened to throw me out of the building.'

'And this is the man who's going to help you?' Grace shook her head. 'Get real, Tom. It's not going to happen. You're going to have to go to the bank again.'

'He came here, didn't he? I didn't ask him to.'

'Curiosity,' said Grace dampeningly. 'I got the impression he was curious, that's all.'

'Well, I'll find out tomorrow,' said Tom, forcing a note of optimism into his voice. 'He's meeting me for lunch at The Crown.'

'Okay.' Grace turned towards the door. 'Well, good luck with Sophie. I wouldn't keep her waiting any longer than you have to, if I was you.'

'So you won't change your mind?'

'I can't.' Grace was definite. 'I'm sorry.' She paused and then added encouragingly, 'Perhaps if you were nice to her, she'd reduce her demands.'

'Not a chance.' Tom was gloomy. 'She wants her pound of flesh and she's determined to have it.' He hesitated a moment and then rounded his desk again, flinging himself into his chair. 'Just spare a thought for me when you're slurping spritzers with your friend.'

CHAPTER THREE

'I'VE got a favour to ask.'

Tom cornered Grace in the kitchen of his house the next morning as she was hurriedly swallowing a cup of tea before leaving for work. She had hoped to avoid Tom and an inevitable discussion of what had gone on the night before. But for once he was up as early as she was, coming into the kitchen in his bathrobe, bare feet squeaking on the tiled floor.

'What is it?' she asked, keeping the width of the pine-blocked table between them. 'You'll have to be quick. I have to open up this morning.'

'I haven't forgotten.' Tom's tone turned a little testy. 'I prepare the schedules, don't I?' Then, as if deciding being short with her wouldn't achieve his ends, he forced a smile. 'I want you to join Oliver and me for lunch.'

Grace almost choked on the last dregs in her cup. 'You have to be joking!'

'No, I'm not.' Tom pushed his hands into the pockets of his robe, apparently uncaring that only a loosely tied belt protected what Grace was sure was his nude body from her gaze. 'I'm not sure he believes me when I say that Sophie and I are finished. If he sees you and me together—'

'No.' Grace was horrified. She really would have to find a place of her own, she thought. Tom was definitely getting the wrong impression of why she'd stayed on after Sophie walked out. 'I don't want to be a party to any deal you make with your brother. And as far as Sophie is concerned, I'm sure she'll see he gets the message for herself.'

Tom's jaw jutted sulkily. 'I notice you haven't asked how I got on last night.'

'It's nothing to do with me,' said Grace desperately. 'Look, I've got to go. It's nearly eight o'clock.'

'She's given me a couple of weeks,' he said, as if Grace hadn't answered him. 'She's as keen as I am to get Oliver involved. That way, she gets her money and possibly the man as well.'

Grace shook her head. 'I don't want to know,' she said, heading for the door. 'I'll see you later.'

'Think about lunch,' Tom advised, not giving up. 'I'd have thought you'd want to save the garden centre as much as me.'

That was a low blow, and Grace's lips tightened for a moment before she said, 'How on earth do you think my presence can make a difference?'

'I've told you.' Tom was encouraged now. 'If he sees us together, he'll think we're an item—'

'But we're not!'

'He needn't know that,' said Tom carelessly, but with the kind of smug expression she most abhorred. He really did think she was interested in him, she thought helplessly. He was so confident of his sex appeal, he assumed it was just a matter of time before she fell into his arms and into his bed.

'I'll think about it,' she murmured, despising her cowardice but deciding she could always cry off later in the morning and avoid a confrontation now. The trouble was, deep down, she was tempted to accept the invitation. It might be the only chance she had of seeing Oliver again.

Apart from helping out around the centre, Grace's main job was in the office. Her degree in maths and her computer skills had enabled her to reorganise the firm's finances, and she was hoping to produce a web site to expand their mail-order sales.

Her fellow workers, a teenage girl who did all the typing and filing, and an older man who had been there since Tom's father was in charge, were gradually beginning to accept her. It occurred to her that if Tom's pursuit of her became unmanageable, she might be forced to leave and she'd be sorry to do that.

The morning was busy. Because of the speed of their turnover, at this time of the year some of their stock had to be brought in from abroad. A huge container truck from Holland arrived with a load of seasonal flowers, and several girls were employed preparing bridal wreaths and bridesmaids' posies for weddings to be held the following day.

Tom arrived about half past nine, smartly attired in a navy suit and crisp white shirt. Obviously for Oliver's benefit, Grace reflected, glancing down at her own jeans and cotton tee shirt with some regret. If she did change her mind and accompanied Tom, she would have to go back to the house to change. The Crown was a fairly casual place, but it wasn't like the coffee shop at the garden centre. There the patrons were mostly older couples and families with young children. They just wanted a snack or a hot drink before heading home.

'I'll be at the site, if anyone wants me,' Tom announced to the office in general, and Gina Robb, who had a crush on him, gave him a provocative smile.

'Want some company?' she asked, edging the neckline of her sweater off one plump shoulder.

Tom grinned. He always liked it when women showed they were attracted to him. 'We wouldn't get much work done if I did,' he responded slyly, and Grace kept her eyes firmly focussed on the computer screen in front of her.

As if sensing her withdrawal, Tom said, 'Everything okay, Grace?' and she was forced to assure him that it was. 'Think any more about lunch?' he continued, and she gritted her teeth. Just the sort of comment Gina wanted to hear.

'Not really,' she said now, looking up. 'Why don't you take Gina instead?'

'Oh, sorry.' He managed to sound suitably regretful as he apologised to the disappointed teenager, though the look he cast in Grace's direction wasn't friendly. 'Grace is the financial genius around here, Gina,' he said. 'I need her expertise. Believe me, you'd be bored out of your skull.'

Gina looked as if boredom would have been the last thing on her agenda and she gave Grace a sulky glare. It probably meant she wasn't going to get much work out of her later, thought Grace irritably. Why couldn't Tom keep his big mouth shut?

'I'll speak to you later, Grace,' he announced, and she resigned herself to the fact that she would have to go with him now. If she didn't, Gina would be offended, and she didn't want to undermine Tom's authority.

At coffee time, when Gina went over to the florists' workroom to gossip with the girls who were preparing the displays, Grace slipped out and drove back to the house. She borrowed Tom's car to speed things up as she'd walked to work as usual.

Parking outside the detached cottage Tom had bought when he and Sophie got together, Grace grabbed her bag and hurried inside. If she was quick, she could be back before anyone missed her.

But what to wear? Surveying her limited wardrobe, Grace was undecided. She seemed to have a predominance of jeans and tee shirts and sweaters, with not much between them and a couple of skimpy dresses more suitable for the evening. Most of her clothes were still at her parents' home in London. She hadn't expected to need power suits for this job.

She eventually plumped for a V-necked black sweater and narrow-legged khaki trousers that flared slightly at the ankle. Teamed with a pair of heeled boots, they would look reasonably smart. Smart enough for The Crown, anyway, she decided, stripping off her tee shirt and jeans and regarding her hips critically. Why did she always think her bottom was bigger than anyone else's?

Did she have time for a shower? She glanced at her watch and assured herself that she did. She could leave what little make-up she wore until later. She'd pop her eye shadow, eyeliner and mascara into her bag.

She was drying herself after her shower when she thought she heard something. Or someone, she reflected nervously, wrapping the towel sarong-wise under her arms. Despite the fact that Tayford was a fairly safe place, Grace had spent enough time in New York and London to feel an immediate sense of anxiety. Had she locked the door when she came in? She suspected she hadn't. But, dammit, surely a thief would see the car and realise that someone was at home.

Opening the bathroom door, she stepped out into her bedroom. Her clothes were still laid out on the bed where she'd left them, together with a clean set of underwear she'd taken out of the drawer. She wanted to put on her bra and panties, but she was loath to shed the towel. She felt absurdly vulnerable without clothes and she was considering dressing in the comparative safety of the bathroom when she heard footsteps on the landing.

Immediately, her heart leapt into her throat. There was somebody else in the house. But who? Could it possibly be Mrs Reynolds, Tom's housekeeper? she wondered hopefully. She didn't usually come in on Fridays, but perhaps Tom had asked her to. He didn't discuss his cleaning arrangements with her.

There was only one way to find out and, deciding that clothes were unlikely to deter a confirmed attacker, she opened her bedroom door a crack. And caught her breath weakly. Tom was outside, on the landing, gazing at her with obvious satisfaction.

'So you are here,' he said, smiling, and she knew at once that this was no coincidental encounter. He must have returned to the office and discovered that both she and his car were missing. It would have needed no great leap of intelligence to guess where she'd gone.

Anger overcame her previous apprehension. 'What are you doing here?' she demanded, and he was left in no doubt she resented his intrusion.

'This is my house,' he said mildly, his smile slipping into a sickly sort of cajolery. 'Come on, Grace. Don't be like that. I'm entitled to come home if I want to.'

Grace's lips tightened. He had a point. 'I'm sorry,' she said stiffly. 'But I got a shock when I heard someone else in the house.' She took a steadying breath. 'Did you forget something?'

'I thought I might take a shower, too,' he said, and Grace's feelings of frustration stirred anew.

'You had a shower this morning,' she reminded him, and Tom shrugged.

'Now I need another,' he said. 'It's dusty at the site. You know that. I don't want to turn up at the pub smelling of cement.'

Grace shrugged. 'Okay.' She withdrew back into her own room. 'I'll see you back at the office.'

'Or we could drive back together,' he suggested as she was closing her door. But Grace chose not to answer him.

It took her exactly four minutes to get dressed. It wasn't until she'd snapped the fastener on her trousers that she felt able to breathe easily again. It was ridiculous, she knew. She slept in the house, for God's sake, and Tom had never intruded on her privacy in the past. Perhaps he did feel grubby after visiting the site. There was a lot of brick dust flying around.

Her hair took slightly longer. She hadn't washed it, but she did brush it out and plait it again. Then, content that she looked as neat as possible, she put her make-up in her bag and left the room.

She was hurrying down the stairs when the doorbell rang. Now what? she wondered grimly. She wanted to get back to the garden centre before Tom reappeared. Wrenching open the door, she prepared to give whatever salesman was on the threshold short shrift, and then felt a hollowing in her stomach at the sight of the man who was standing outside.

Why Oliver Ferreira should have this effect on her, she didn't know. It wasn't as if he'd shown any particular interest in her. After all, as soon as his ex-wife had appeared, he'd forgotten all about her.

Yet, just the sight of his lean dark face and muscled body and she was struggling to control feelings she hardly recognised. A navy blue shirt under a dark blue suit complemented his brooding sensuality, and she knew the craziest need to reach out and touch him, as if she couldn't quite believe that he was real. But he was real enough, she knew, as dark eyes shaded by sinfully long lashes appraised her in a way that made her nerves tingle. Oh, God, she thought, feeling her skin moisten in response, he was even more attractive than she remembered.

'Grace,' he said, in obvious surprise, and although she was flattered that he remembered her name, the frown drawing his dark brows together was hardly encouraging. And, instantly, she knew what he was thinking. Thank goodness he hadn't arrived any sooner and found her only half dressed.

'Hi,' she said. She sounded breathless, she thought unhappily. She hoped he wouldn't attribute that to his sudden appearance. 'Um—have you come from the garden centre?'

'I was looking for Tom, actually,' he said, without really

answering her. Then his eyes moved past her to the stairs behind her.

'And you've found him,' declared Tom, and she glanced almost disbelievingly over her shoulder. Tom was coming down the stairs, clad only in a towel. 'Come in, Oliver,' he said cheerfully. 'Did Bill tell you we were here?'

Grace perched on a stool at the bar sipping her iced tea through a straw. Tom and Oliver were standing nearby, each holding a glass. Tom's lager, Oliver's Diet Coke. Oliver had hardly touched his, she noticed. He'd only agreed to have it to be polite, she was sure.

For her part, Grace would have loved to order a Bacardi and Coke, just to lift her spirits. The day had been going downhill ever since she'd made that crack about Tom bringing Gina to the pub. Now she was here at The Crown, wishing the floor would just open up and swallow her. Oliver had hardly spoken a word to her since Tom's embarrassing entrance. And who could blame him? The implications of that 'we' and the fact that she and Tom had been at the house in the middle of the day were too gruesome to contemplate.

She hunched her shoulders, feeling humiliated. She'd had no conception that Oliver might come to the house looking for his brother. Or that Tom would appear, half naked, giving weight to any suspicions Oliver might have. He probably hadn't known she was still sharing Tom's house. Though that was one little titbit Sophie would have loved to share.

Perhaps she had, Grace reflected gloomily. Perhaps she was only kidding herself that Oliver had seemed taken aback when she'd answered the door. And on top of everything else, why should he care? She was sure he hadn't been lonely for female company since Sophie walked out.

She tried to tune into what Oliver and Tom were talking

about. It seemed they were discussing the weather, ludi-crous as that was. She wondered when Tom was going to get round to the real point of this meeting. If she were Oliver she wouldn't buy Tom's air of *bonhomie* for a min-ute.

'Your table's ready, Mr Ferreira.'

The waitress from the pub's dining room appeared just as Grace was considering making an excuse and leaving, and Tom nodded his thanks before emptying his glass. Oliver, meanwhile, put his untouched Coke on the bar and held out his hand to help her down from the bar stool. For a moment, his cool fingers gripped her arm and her eyes darted to his. But he wasn't looking at her and he clearly felt none of the heat that spread along her veins at his touch.

The dining room wasn't busy. It was early yet, barely half past twelve, but it had been obvious from the start that Oliver had wanted to get this meeting over and done with. Grace guessed that was why he'd come to the house when Tom wasn't at the garden centre. Perhaps he'd hoped to avoid a formal gathering at somewhere public like The Crown.

Whatever, Tom had been having none of it and he'd insisted Oliver come back to the centre and see for himself how successful it was. Consequently, Oliver had driven Tom back in his car, while Grace had taken the Volvo, as before.

But for the remainder of the morning the situation had not been ideal. Oliver had renewed his acquaintance with the members of staff who'd been there since his father's tenure, and Tom had done his best to behave as if he weren't facing financial ruin. Grace, meanwhile, had tried to concentrate on the web site she was designing. The idea was to expand Ferreira's mail-order business by advertising online.

They were seated at a table in the window. Menus were

produced and Grace regarded the choice of entrées with a heavy heart. She wasn't hungry. Indeed, if she was honest she felt physically revolted at the thought of food. She couldn't bear to look at Tom's deceitful face and not remember the deliberate way he'd tried to mislead his brother.

'What are you having?' To her annoyance, Tom leaned towards her and examined the menu over her shoulder. 'The steak and kidney pie is good,' he said. 'I can recommend it. Or the rack of lamb. It's locally produced, you know.'

Grace managed to control the urge to put some space between them and gave a shrug. 'I just want a salad,' she said. 'I'm used to just having a sandwich at lunchtime.'

'All the more reason to splash out today,' declared Tom, clearly not getting the message. 'Go on. The business can afford it.' He paused, and then added significantly, 'Or it could if Oliver's wife wasn't trying to bankrupt me.'

Grace cast an agonised look in Oliver's direction. But although she'd expected him to say something, even if it was only that Sophie was his *ex*-wife, he continued to study the menu without commenting.

'I think I'll have a burger,' he said at last, and now his dark gaze did meet Grace's briefly. But there was no liking there, no warmth at all. Just a dismissive contempt that chilled her to the bone.

'Oh, but, hey, is nobody going to have a starter?' Tom protested. 'This is supposed to be a social occasion. You're both behaving as if we're eating at the local fast-food joint.'

'Perhaps we should be,' remarked Oliver, speaking at last, though clearly not saying what his brother wanted to hear. 'If, as you're implying, you're on the verge of bankruptcy—'

'The business isn't on the verge of bankruptcy,' Tom

snapped angrily. 'And you know it. If you'd just look at the books—'

'Have you decided what you're going to have?'

The waitress who had shown them to the table was now standing beside them, her notepad raised expectantly, and both men were forced to abandon their discussion in favour of choosing what they wanted to eat. Grace picked a ham salad and Oliver did as he'd said he was going to do and ordered a burger. It meant that Tom had to choose something similar in deference to his guests.

'Would you like anything to drink?'

The waitress clearly handled the drinks order, too, and Tom looked reflectively at Oliver and Grace. Then, with an impatient exclamation, he said, 'Just a bottle of sparkling mineral water, Stacey, thanks.' His lips twisted sardonically. 'Must keep a clear head for business.'

The waitress left and Grace assumed an intense interest in her place-mat. She really didn't want to be here, she thought, wondering why she'd ever agreed to come. Somehow, appeasing Tom had lost its imperative. She didn't even know why he wanted her here. Not when his brother obviously resented her company.

'Have you heard when Mum and Dad are coming home?' asked Oliver into the awkward silence that had fallen, and Tom gave him a brooding look.

'Dad can't bail me out, if that's what you're thinking,' he said shortly. 'We're not all money magnets like you. He's had a few dodgy investments lately. You know what the share market's been like. Last I heard, he was thinking of selling the villa in San Luis and buying a condo in one of those holiday complexes instead.'

Grace saw Oliver's brows draw together. 'You're not serious.'

'Why not? Lots of people do it. Especially people who're getting on like Mum and Dad.'

Oliver's jaw tightened. 'Dad would hate living in a condo, and you know it. Half his pleasure in owning the villa is the land it stands on. He's a gardener, Tom, not a beach bum!'

Tom shrugged. 'That's not my problem.'

Oliver stared at him. 'He's your father!'

'And you're my brother, and a lot of good that's done me.'

Oliver's eyes narrowed. 'Are you saying this is my fault?'

At last Tom had the decency to hang his head, but his words were grudging. 'No,' he muttered. 'Not exactly. But you should have warned me about Sophie. Goddammit, you must have known what she was like.'

Grace didn't know where to look. It was bad enough being present at what was, essentially, a family meeting. It was much worse having to listen to Tom discuss his brother's personal affairs in public.

Whatever he thought, however he felt, Oliver had been married to Sophie for six years. And judging by the way he'd behaved the day before, he still cared about her.

Oliver was regarding his brother almost humorously now, a look of mild amazement on his face. 'So I was supposed to warn the man who'd been screwing my wife that she wasn't to be trusted,' he remarked thoughtfully. 'Have you forgotten where she got the money to invest in the business, or did you think I sold my house because I couldn't bear the unhappy associations it held?'

Tom flushed then, his fair features looking older suddenly. 'You could afford it,' he muttered, glowering at the waitress who had arrived with the bottled water. 'I can't.'

Oliver waited until the woman had filled everyone's glass and left again before responding. 'I couldn't afford it,' he told Tom forcefully. 'She took half of everything I had. Why do you think I live in a loft apartment? It taught me never to trust a woman again.'

Tom gave a scornful sniff and Grace, who had hoped that would be an end of it, closed her eyes. She dreaded to think what Oliver must be thinking at that moment. If Tom had intended to pay her back for what she'd said earlier, he had certainly succeeded.

'We all know that's no ordinary apartment,' Tom persisted, and she stifled an inward groan. 'I wish I could afford to live on Myer's Wharf.'

Oliver's expression hardened. 'Where I live isn't relevant,' he said as the waitress returned with their burgers and salad. 'I'm sure Grace is fed up with listening to us arguing.' He looked down at his plate with apparent enthusiasm. 'Mmm, this looks good.'

Grace flashed him a grateful smile, but she wasn't sure he noticed, or that he particularly cared what she thought. Still, she desperately hoped the food would keep Tom's mouth occupied long enough for her to eat a little of her salad. Perhaps she could excuse herself before they offered coffee. She could always get a taxi back to the garden centre.

But she should have known better, she reflected. 'So you're determined not to help me out,' Tom demanded, his jaw set in a belligerent scowl. He pointed a stubby finger at his brother. 'I just hope you can sleep nights when the business goes to the wall.'

'Hold it right there.' Oliver had apparently had enough, and although the glance he cast in Grace's direction was impatient, he didn't hesitate before going on. 'You chose the life you have now, so get over it. It's not my fault if it's kicked you in the b—teeth!'

Tom grunted then and pushed his plate aside, almost knocking his water over as he did so. 'I'm going to the loo,' he announced loudly and Grace guessed that everyone in the room must have heard what he said. 'You speak to him, Gracie. Try and get it through his thick head that I'm not the bastard he thinks I am.'

CHAPTER FOUR

SO MUCH for having a drink—Diet Coke, of course—and getting out of there before things got personal, thought Oliver wryly. Why the hell had he turned up at the garden centre at ten-thirty? Why hadn't he just come to the pub at lunchtime as they'd arranged?

He knew why, of course. The reason was sitting opposite him. Grace Lovell, whose warm beauty and curvaceous body had haunted his dreams.

She was just as beautiful as he'd imagined. Those dark-fringed green eyes and glorious hair were only accentuated by the sweater she was wearing. He would like to see her hair loose, he thought, a red-gold stream of silk across a pillow. His pillow, he acknowledged, with a twist of irony. Were he and Tom destined to want the same women?

But, no. He banished that thought before it had time to develop. He was attracted to Grace Lovell, yes, but he had no intention of acting on it. It was obvious, as Sophie had contended, that she and his brother were an item. If he'd had any doubts on that score, they'd been dispelled when he'd found them together at Tom's house.

'I'm sorry,' she said suddenly, and Oliver realised she was apologising for his brother.

'I'm sorry, too,' he said politely. There was no reason to fall out with her just because Tom was a fool. He glanced about him. 'Is this where you and Tom usually have lunch?'

And that was just one step better than, Do you come here often? he thought with an inward groan. He wasn't surprised when she gave him an old-fashioned look.

'No,' she said. 'I usually have a sandwich in the coffee

46

shop.' She paused. 'I suppose you go out for lunch with clients all the time.'

'No way.' Oliver was stung by her casual assumption that he spent his days entertaining customers. He glanced towards the door Tom had exited by, saw there was no sign of his brother and heaved a sigh. 'Sure, there are times when I'm forced to offer hospitality to clients. But I don't spend all my time sucking up to them.'

She looked at him through her lashes and he wondered if she realised how provocative that was. 'I can't imagine you sucking up to anyone,' she told him, slightly breath- lessly, and he felt himself harden at the realisation that she was flirting with him.

And he could imagine himself sucking up to her, he thought impatiently. Or rather, sucking her, he amended, his eyes flickering over the round breasts outlined by the tight sweater. He could almost imagine what she'd taste like, her nipples hard and swollen against his tongue. Her skin would be soft and, because she was hot, maybe a little salty. Though she couldn't be as hot as he was, he thought, adjusting his tight trousers with a surreptitious hand.

'You're not like Tom at all,' she murmured suddenly. 'He's younger than you, isn't he?' She met his wary gaze. 'Maybe that's why he feels the need to compete.'

'Does he? Compete, I mean?' Oliver was interested to know where this was going. Had Tom left her here to soften him up? He wouldn't put it past him. He'd do anything, use any situation, to get his own way.

'I think so.' But her eyes dropped away and she picked uninterestedly at her salad to avoid looking at him again. The tip of a pink tongue appeared to moisten her upper lip. 'But he can't, and he knows it. You're the successful one and he envies you.'

'Really?' Oliver was sardonic. 'I suppose that was why he seduced my wife and encouraged her to get a divorce.'

'Maybe.' A faint hint of colour touched her cheeks. 'If she was capable of being seduced, perhaps the marriage wasn't working anyway,' she ventured reasonably. 'The way I hear it, you were never around when she needed you.'

'Sophie is a needy person,' said Oliver drily, not much caring what she made of that. He knew what he meant and it wasn't flattering. But he had no intention of sharing that with Tom's latest squeeze.

Grace looked up then. 'And you're not?'

'I'm not what?' Oliver stared at her.

'A needy person,' she answered huskily, and he wondered suddenly what else she'd heard about him.

'If this is some roundabout way of telling me that you know I have a drink problem, then say so,' he exclaimed harshly. 'I'm not ashamed to admit it. When my marriage broke up, I went to pieces for a while.'

Grace's face was red now. 'I didn't mean that,' she said, but he noticed she didn't deny being aware of what had happened. How could she not? he thought bitterly. It must have been hot gossip, not just in Tayford, but in San Luis as well.

'Yeah, right.' He lifted his shoulders and then let them fall dismissively. It had happened too long ago for him to feel embarrassed about it now. He considered his words before he spoke, and then said drily, 'I dare say you agree with Sophie. You evidently know Tom very well.'

Grace frowned. 'I don't know about Sophie, but of course I know Tom. He was kind enough to offer me this job without asking for any qualifications at all.'

'Good for Tom.' Oliver was sardonic. 'He's obviously a much more attractive character than me.'

'You don't mean that.' Grace flashed him a defensive look. 'You're a very attractive man and you know it. I think so, anyway.'

Oliver was taken aback at first. But then he realised what was going on. 'I guess this is the real reason Tom brought you along,' he said, deciding his first estimate had been correct. 'Has he gone to the men's room to give you time to use your powers of persuasion to make me change my mind?'

'No!' Grace looked horrified and Oliver thought she was either a very good actress or she genuinely meant it. 'If you must know,' she retorted tersely, 'he wanted you to believe we were together. So you'd accept the fact that he's not interested in your ex-wife.'

'Oh, I know he's not interested in Sophie,' replied Oliver evenly, pushing his plate aside and regarding her with a sceptical gaze.

Grace absorbed this, looking slightly puzzled. 'All right,' she said at last. 'So I got that wrong.' She waited a beat and then she went on carefully, 'And I can understand you feeling bitter. You and Sophie had been married for a long time.'

Oliver felt irritated suddenly. He didn't want her sympathy. Once again, he had the suspicion that her words were a deliberate attempt to gain ground. 'I'm not bitter,' he said, and he realised it was true. He wasn't. 'Like you say, there were probably faults on both sides.'

Grace hesitated. 'You—didn't have any children?'

'No.' Oliver's lips thinned. 'I guess that's another strike against me.'

'Didn't you want a family?'

Oliver snorted. 'I think that's my business, don't you?'

Grace bent her head, the sweater's loose neckline slipping off one creamy shoulder. 'I'd like a family,' she said, her voice low and disruptively intimate. 'Being an only child is no fun, believe me.'

Once again, Oliver was disturbed by the images her words created. He could imagine her having a baby, her slim frame swollen with the child she was bearing. Tom's child, he told himself, determinedly banishing any other alternative that presented itself. Though whether his brother would make a good father was anyone's guess.

'I'm sure you'll get what you want,' he said now, glancing towards the exit again, wondering where the hell his brother had gone. He wouldn't put it past him to walk out. But if he did, he was forfeiting the chance to pursue his demands.

'Do you think you'll marry again?'

Grace seemed determined to get him to talk about himself and Oliver looked at her levelly. 'Not if I have anything to do with it,' he said, not caring how unfeeling that sounded. 'I'm thinking of following my brother's example. Why buy a book yourself when you can join a library?'

'You won't do that.' Her face showed none of the outrage he'd expected. 'As I told you before, you're not like Tom.'

'I could be. You don't know me.'

'No.' She acknowledged that. 'But if you were, you wouldn't have accused me of coming on to you. Not that I was coming on to you,' she added hastily. 'But if I had been, you'd have taken me up on it.'

Oliver couldn't help being intrigued by her candour. 'You're saying I should have behaved like Tom and attempted to seduce his girlfriend?' He shook his head. 'I'm not quite as predictable as that.'

Her green eyes narrowed. 'Why not?' He had the feeling she was fighting the urge to find out. But then, as if she couldn't help herself, 'Don't you find me attractive?'

Oliver stifled the retort that sprang to his lips. He had no intention of giving Tom that satisfaction. And then, to his relief, he saw his brother coming back to their table and any response was mute.

'Coffee?' he said, as if that were the only thought in his

head, and Tom grunted an acknowledgement as he dropped back into his seat.

'Why not?' he said, giving Grace an inquiring look. 'We're in no hurry, are we, babe?'

'You may not be,' she retorted, surprising both men as she got to her feet and gathered up her bag and jacket. Avoiding Oliver's eyes, she added crisply, 'It was nice to talk to you, Mr Ferreira. Tom, I'll see you back at the office, okay?'

Mr Ferreira?

Oliver was still digesting this when Tom stumbled to his feet to offer a protest, causing him to wonder exactly where his brother had been during his prolonged absence. Not in the men's room, Oliver would bet.

'You can't do that,' Tom exclaimed in a low impassioned voice as Oliver reluctantly vacated his chair also. 'You don't have any transport.'

'I can get a taxi,' Grace declared, heading for the door, and Oliver was forced to accept that he couldn't follow her example when Tom slumped back into his seat.

In the event, Grace walked back to the garden centre. It was easier than hanging about the foyer of the pub waiting for a lift, running the risk of the brothers deciding to abandon the lunch and joining her. Right at this moment she'd have been happy if she never had to see either of them again, and that was stupid. Worse, it was pathetic. She'd never made such a fool of herself before and she just wanted to find somewhere safe so she could lick her wounds in private.

She gave an inward groan at the memory of her blunder. Had she really asked Oliver if he found her attractive? God, how pitiful was that? It had been painfully obvious what he thought of her and attractive didn't begin to cover it.

As for Tom, she cringed again at the way he had behaved. Oliver must have thought he was lunching with a pair of morons and her presence had been integral to that impression.

It was over a mile back to the garden centre and by the time she got there, Grace's ankles were aching. She hadn't expected to walk far in the high-heeled boots and they were definitely not meant for hiking along country roads whose surface was uneven to say the least. In addition to which, she had attempted to conceal herself in the hedge every time a car had passed going in the same direction, desperate to avoid any further humiliation.

Gina eyed her speculatively when she limped into the office fifteen minutes later, but evidently her expression deterred even the cocky teenager from making any comment. Instead, Grace was allowed to make her way to her desk in silence where she indulged herself by taking off the offending boots and cooling her burning soles against the carpet tiles. Bliss, she thought ruefully. If only all her troubles could be cured as easily.

It infuriated her that Tom apparently already knew his brother was assured that he and Sophie were no longer together. If that was so, why on earth had he insisted that she join them for lunch?

She knew, of course. One way or another, Tom was giving the impression that she was interested in him. And she wasn't. She never had been. Oh, when she'd first got to know him, she'd liked him well enough. He'd been fun to be with and she'd thought he was like his father, a bluff, genial man who liked nothing so much as to get his hands into the rich, loamy soil he'd created.

But Tom wasn't like George Ferreira. The garden centre was just a means to an end. He wanted to be as successful as his brother and, as he didn't have the brains to follow him to university, he'd used a tenuous interest in gardening to persuade his father to leave the centre to him.

Of course, she hadn't known that when he offered her this job. She'd been really grateful for the opportunity it had given her to get out of teaching. She still was. But gratitude was all it was. Not some latent desire to take Sophie's place. Until she'd met Oliver Ferreira, she'd believed she didn't want another man in her life.

Her lips tightened as she brought the web site she was designing up on the computer screen. Hold that thought, she mused grimly, studying the graphics she'd designed for the banner headline of the site without enthusiasm. Her experience with men, little though it was, had not been particularly successful. Why did she think Oliver Ferreira was any different from the other guys she'd dated? Being beautiful, she'd discovered, without any false modesty, seemed to create more problems than it solved.

And she could just imagine how Tom would react if he discovered she'd been flirting with his brother. He'd be sure to think the worst, sure to get the wrong idea. But, she reminded herself severely, that wasn't going to be a problem. Oliver had made it painfully clear that he considered her—and her behaviour—an embarrassment.

She'd just managed to assure herself that she wasn't going to worry about it when Tom came stamping into the office. As it was almost an hour since she'd left them at The Crown, Grace hoped the rest of the meeting had been more successful than before she'd left. But one look at her employer's face was enough to disabuse her of that wish, and his, 'Come into my office, Grace,' was issued without any apparent consideration for the work she was doing.

Even Gina looked sympathetic when Grace was forced to ease her aching feet back into her boots and leave her computer. She limped across the office, trying to suppress her own feelings of resentment. But, dammit, she hadn't wanted to have lunch with him and his brother in the first place.

'Shut the door.'

Tom's tone was brusque, but Grace only pushed the door part way, refusing to obey his orders slavishly. Besides, if he was going to fire her, she wanted Bill and Gina to hear it. She didn't know much about unfair dismissals, but the term 'sexual harassment' seemed fairly apt.

Tom had flung himself into the chair behind his desk and was now regarding her mulishly. 'Why the hell did you run out on me like that?' he demanded, without any preamble. 'What did he say to you? If he insulted you, I'll break his bloody neck!'

Yeah, right.

Grace thought it would take someone far bigger and far stronger to break Oliver Ferreira's neck, but she kept her thoughts to herself. 'No,' she said, standing in front of the desk instead of sitting down. 'He was very—nice, actually. Very polite.'

'So this pillar of politeness said nothing to offend your sensibilities?'

'No.'

'So do you mind telling me why you charged out of the Crown as if Old Nick himself was at your heels?'

'I didn't.' But she knew she had, and she was going to need a far better excuse than that she'd wanted to get back to work to satisfy him. She moistened her lips to give herself time to marshal an argument. 'Um—I just felt in the way,' she offered at last. 'You'd been gone—it seemed like for ever, and we—that is, Oliver and I, had nothing to say to one another.'

Tom looked sceptical. 'You must have talked about something.'

'Well, we did. To begin with, anyway.' Then she realised how she could get out of this. 'But where were you, for heaven's sake? And don't pretend you spent the whole twenty minutes in the loo!'

Now it was Tom's turn to look discomfited. 'Okay, okay,' he said defensively. 'I admit it. I went into the bar.' He pulled a face. 'Why wouldn't I? That bastard was enjoying my humiliation.'

'I don't think that's entirely true.' Grace couldn't let him get away with slandering his brother. 'I told you it was unreasonable to expect Oliver to bail you out. You've barely spoken to him in over four years.'

'And your point is?'

'You know what my point is, Tom.' Respecting his privacy, she leaned back against the door until it closed with a definite click. 'You got yourself into this mess. Now, you've got to get yourself out of it. Talk to Sophie again. Ask her if she'll give you more time.'

'You know what she said last night. I told you,' retorted Tom dourly. 'While you were out, enjoying yourself.'

Grace wouldn't have called a meal in a fast-food restaurant and a mediocre film enjoying herself, exactly, but she didn't contradict him. 'Well, two weeks is a start,' she said brightly. 'And surely after living together for so long, she still has some affection for you.'

'Sophie only has affection for herself.' Tom was vehement. 'She doesn't care who she hurts as long as she gets what she wants. She wants Oliver back again, I know that. I pity him if he takes her up on it.'

CHAPTER FIVE

OLIVER asked the waiter for the cheque, wondering why the evening had not been as enjoyable as he had hoped.

All the ingredients for a successful evening were there: an intimate restaurant, whose soft lighting and blues quartet playing all his favourite jazz had created the right atmosphere; good wine and good food, prepared by one of the country's top chefs; but, not least, the companionship of a woman he had known and liked for the past six months, and whom, until recently, he had seriously been considering making a pe.manent part of his life.

Not that marriage had been in his plans. He believed he and Miranda understood one another, and their relationship had always been based on friendship and compatibility as well as sex. She was a company lawyer, who had trained in London and was now working in Newcastle. Like him, she was a divorcée, and after meeting at a cocktail party his partner, Andy Faulkner, had hosted, they'd discovered they had other interests in common.

But somehow the evening had turned sour. Although they'd previously shared a love of classical music, he'd found himself arguing with her over the merits of a performance of an opera they'd seen the week before. And despite their mutual interest in art and painting, he'd spent at least part of the evening finding excuses why he couldn't attend a Turner seascapes exhibition that Miranda had been lucky enough to get tickets for.

The account settled, they emerged into the cool, rain-spattered air to find a taxi waiting for them. Oliver had had the waiter call the local service while he was settling his bill, and Miranda hurried across the pavement eagerly to step inside the cab.

Oliver accompanied her, helping her inside with a courteous hand. But although she evidently expected him to join her, he demurred.

'I think I'll walk home,' he said, knowing as he voiced the words that he was, in essence, ending the evening there and then. Miranda would have been expecting him to accompany her home, and in other circumstances that was exactly what he would have done. And spent the night in her very comfortable apartment, he conceded. So why did that prospect suddenly seem so unattractive?

'All right,' she said in response, but he could tell by her tone that she was hurt. And curious, too, he guessed ruefully. She was probably wondering what was going on.

'I'll ring you tomorrow,' he said, leaning forward to kiss her lips briefly before closing the cab door. He lifted a hand as the car drove away. 'Goodnight.'

It was a good mile and a half to his quayside apartment, but he wasn't worried. The walk would do him good, he thought. It might help to clear his head and maybe understand what it was that was bugging him. It wasn't what he'd had to drink. Although he always bought wine for Miranda, he'd only swallowed half a glass. But something very definitely had him on edge.

It was easy to blame Tom for his present state of uncertainty. Meeting his brother again, learning of his breakup with Sophie, should have put things in perspective, but it hadn't. Oh, he now knew why Tom had come to see him. Why he'd made such a big thing of his and Sophie's separation and the money she'd invested in the business. Yet, despite the suspicion that Tom might have done him a favour by exposing his ex-wife's failings, Oliver still felt bitter. And it was what had happened at lunch three days ago that persisted in distracting his mind.

And there he had it, he thought, striding aggressively along the lamp-lit street, his whole demeanour warning any would-be mugger from trying his luck. Not that there were many people about. The quickening rain had deterred all but the most hardy pedestrians. Thinking about where he might have been at that moment—where he should have been were it not for his bad mood—he wondered why he didn't feel more guilty. But the truth was, he didn't want Miranda's company at this moment. Not when another woman's image was filling his thoughts.

Grace Lovell.

He scowled. He must be out of his head, and he knew it. But the fact was, he'd had the devil's own job thinking of anything else for the past two days. It hadn't been quite as bad over the weekend. Andy Faulkner had roped him into a pro-am golf tournament on Saturday, and although Oliver was no enthusiast, he'd enjoyed the company; and on Sunday he'd gone into the office to catch up on his correspondence and had found other work to do.

Miranda hadn't objected. She'd told him she was putting the finishing touches to a brief that was coming to court in the next few days, and they'd agreed not to see one another until Monday night. But now he'd gone and spoiled their reunion, and it would serve him right if she ditched him and found someone else.

The annoying thing was that that idea didn't disturb him as it should have done. Dammit, a week ago, he'd actually considered asking her to move in with him, and now he was thinking of a possible severance of their relationship with no real regret. No, that wasn't true, he argued irritably. He would miss Miranda if she decided their affair was over. During the past six months they'd become very close.

But not close enough, a small voice chided mockingly. Or he wouldn't be considering their breakup so objectively. Perhaps he was simply not the kind of man to get involved with. Sophie had certainly thought so, until she'd had this miraculous change of heart.

But it wasn't Sophie who was making him feel so unsettled, so frustrated. He wondered what the hell Grace had meant by asking him if he found her attractive. Wasn't one man enough for her either? Dear God, she must know perfectly well that he found her attractive. Physically, anyway. He'd bet any number of men had speculated on what she'd be like in bed. As he had, he conceded, despising the admission. Only in his case, he had no intention of doing anything about it.

Nevertheless, finding her and Tom together at the house had really thrown him. How often did they make time for a quickie in the middle of the morning? Or at any other time of day, for that matter? It seemed Sophie hadn't been exaggerating when she'd said they were an item. He'd had no reason not to believe her, of course, but until Friday morning he had hoped she was wrong.

Remembering his reaction when Grace had opened the door, he felt a surge of anger at his own disillusionment. He didn't need a crystal ball to know what they'd been doing. That was why she'd appeared so flushed when she'd opened the door. She'd even had the grace—he excused himself the pun—to look slightly shamefaced when his brother appeared behind her. And Tom had looked so bloody smug, Oliver had wanted to bury his fist in the other man's face.

Of course, he hadn't. They'd all been excessively civilised about it, Tom disappearing again to get dressed, and Grace offering him a cup of coffee while he waited, which he'd declined. In all honesty, he'd wanted nothing so much as to get out of there, out of that house. It was the house where Tom had taken his ex-wife, for heaven's sake. He should never have gone there. He wouldn't make that mistake again.

He paused above Vicker's Wharf, looking down on the proposed new development. At night, the quayside was a blaze of lights, the luxury apartments fronting the river looking cosmopolitan and slightly out of place. Where warehouses had once stood, there was now a huge entertainment arena, and plans for its further expansion were already in the pipeline.

His own apartment on Myer's Wharf had not yet been overtaken by the city planners. Although the warehouse below was empty, there were still businesses struggling to survive farther along the quay. He let himself in on the ground floor and stepped into the commercial lift that served the building. His was the only apartment here, but he usually appreciated the privacy and isolation it gave him.

Tonight, however, he was restless. Stepping out of the lift into the huge space that served as both a living room and kitchen, he didn't feel the usual pleasure in his surroundings. Locking the double doors that successfully secured the lift in place, he crossed the darkened room to the long floor-to-ceiling windows. Outside the river was a wide black ribbon, dark and driven. Like himself, he thought contemptuously. Hadn't he learned anything in his thirty-four years of life?

He'd suspected something was wrong, of course, when Tom came to see him. But his brother had convinced him that the garden centre was thriving, and it was. However, although he'd known Sophie had invested in it, he'd never dreamt Tom had allowed her to sink all her capital in the business. The fact that they'd separated wouldn't have made a difference in normal circumstances. But it was natural Sophie would need some funds to get an apartment of her own.

It seemed, however, that Sophie wasn't prepared to compromise. She wanted out, immediately, and Oliver guessed there was a little revenge in her demands. And why not?

She must be feeling aggrieved that Tom had found someone else to take her place. It was natural that she'd be jealous. He didn't buy all that crap about her wishing she'd never left him. Sophie had always done what she wanted, and it must bug her to no end that this time she'd been duped.

He gritted his teeth. It bugged him, too. And Tom bringing Grace Lovell to lunch with them had seemed like a deliberate attempt to prove that he had no secrets from her. What really sickened Oliver was the way Tom had left her to attempt to sweeten his demands. Had he expected her to try and seduce him? How far was he prepared to go to get the investment he needed?

How far was she?

Oliver quashed that thought, turning from the windows in disgust, but it refused to go away. What was he thinking? he wondered. Was he considering giving Tom the cash he needed on the basis of favours granted?

No!

He strode into the kitchen and swung open one of the doors on the double-size fridge-freezer and yanked out a bottle of diet soda. The illumination from inside the cabinet lit his face briefly, and he glimpsed his reflection in the stainless steel door of the oven. He looked driven, he thought, not liking the analogy. Driven, and frustrated, and how pathetic was that?

He awoke at six, his body bathed in sweat, the covers twisted shroud-like about his naked body. He'd been dreaming, and he didn't need to think hard to know what he'd been dreaming about.

Grace!

Flinging himself onto his back, he raked savage hands through his damp, tumbled hair, feeling the familiar pangs of frustration knifing through his loins. He didn't need to see the tented sheet to know he was hard and aroused by the emotions his unconscious mind had generated, his head still filled with images of her slim body spread-eagled beneath him, her hands cool and delicious against his hot flesh.

God!

With a groan of disgust, Oliver tore the covers aside and pushed himself up from the bed. Then, after dropping the quilt on the floor, he methodically stripped the huge bed of its sheets and dumped them in the laundry basket in his bathroom. His housekeeper, Mrs Jackson, would make her own assessment of his reasons for doing so, hopefully not the real ones.

The underfloor heating hadn't yet kicked in and, although to begin with he had appreciated the chill of the apartment, now he felt cold. Grabbing the towelling robe from the back of the bathroom door, he slid his arms into the sleeves, tightening the sash about his waist as he went into the kitchen.

After setting a pot of coffee to filter, he leaned back against a granite-topped unit and tipped back his head against the oak-panelled door above. His shoulders ached, probably from fighting the sheets half the night, and his eyes felt prickly from lack of sleep. Well, restful sleep, anyway, he amended drily, trying to find some humour in the situation and failing abysmally. There was nothing remotely humorous about his present situation and he knew it.

This was all Tom's fault, he thought grimly, needing a scapegoat and finding it in his brother. If Tom hadn't turned up at the office, if he hadn't insisted on making a scene so that Oliver had been obliged to arrange an alternative venue, he'd never have gone to the garden centre.

And if he hadn't gone to the garden centre, he might never have laid eyes on Grace Lovell, never found himself lusting after a woman who made Sophie's transgressions seem almost forgivable by comparison. Sophie had been weak and selfish; Grace was both strong and determined. She was prepared to do just about anything to get what she wanted.

He scowled. He knew that was a hopeless simplification of the situation. His attraction to Grace had been urgent and instantaneous and owed nothing to anyone else's faults but his own. Okay, without Tom's intervention he might never have met her, but it wasn't his brother's fault that he found himself entertaining such erotic dreams about her. Indeed, if Tom had any inkling of the things he was thinking about Grace, he would probably blow his top.

Or would he? Oliver realised he had no real idea what Tom thought about his mistress. Yes, he had enjoyed rubbing Oliver's nose in the fact that they were sleeping together, but beyond that he was totally in the dark. Did Tom think he was in love with her? Oliver's lips twisted. All his life, his brother had been very good at convincing himself he was in love with a long stream of women, the last of which just happened to be Oliver's wife.

Personally, Oliver thought that being 'in love' was a self-deluding fantasy. He'd thought he was in love with Sophie, but time, and the acknowledgement of his own failings, had convinced him that sex had played the biggest part in his fascination with her. The fact that she'd refused to go to bed with him until after they were married had been a powerful incentive and he'd been fool enough to believe that once his ring was on her finger, all their problems would be over.

Of course, it hadn't been like that. Oh, she'd still been a virgin. She hadn't been lying about that. But he'd soon discovered that it hadn't been hard for her to deny herself that indulgence.

Nevertheless, he'd still convinced himself that so long as

they loved one another, that was the most important thing. He'd been twenty-four, for God's sake! What had he really known about life? These days, he was firmly convinced that he'd been as much a virgin in his way as she'd been in hers. But for different reasons.

Six years on, he'd had a rude awakening. Sophie's affair with Tom had briefly robbed him of any confidence he'd had in himself and for a while he'd wallowed in self-pity. He recognised it as that now and, thankfully, it hadn't lasted. By the time he'd emerged from the Abbey, he'd been a wiser, and more cynical, man.

Yet, even so, it had taken four years for him to realise that what he'd felt for Sophie had been as much self-delusion as reality. Even his affair with Miranda hadn't totally banished Sophie's image. It wasn't until he'd seen Grace, until he'd met her and talked to her, that he'd real-ised his infatuation with the illusion he'd had of his marriage was well and truly over.

So perhaps Tom did deserve some credit for that. After all, he had taken Sophie off his hands, and if he was now discovering she wasn't the financial pushover he'd imag-ined, that wasn't Oliver's problem.

Even so, he wouldn't like to see his father's business fall into bankruptcy, Oliver reflected, pouring himself a mug of the aromatic brew he had made. Taking a sip of the strong black coffee, he inhaled its fragrance and felt the reassuring kick of caffeine invade his system.

Then, carrying the mug through to his living room, he acknowledged that if he could do anything to ease his fa-ther's burden—including preventing him from having to sell the villa in Spain, which had been his life's aspiration, to move into a condo—he should do it. He knew the old man was just quixotic enough to bankrupt himself to bail out his younger son, and Oliver couldn't let him do that. Not if he could supply an alternative.

And he could, he conceded, walking across to the windows, pushing his free hand into the pocket of his robe. Remembering the last statement his accountant had sent him, he knew he could, without too much difficulty, free up the funds to secure both the garden centre and his father's villa—if the old man would let him.

Perhaps he ought to take a trip out to Spain and speak to his father himself, he considered thoughtfully. He'd only ever visited the villa once, always making excuses about being too busy or having too many professional commitments to make the trip. In truth, he'd been avoiding his mother's sympathy. Mrs Ferreira had never forgiven Sophie for betraying him with his brother, without realising that Oliver would have preferred to consign that affair to the past.

He supposed it had been hard for his mother not to take sides, and his own behaviour had hardly reassured her. He'd allowed the whole business to assume much too large a place in his life. It was time he told her how he felt now, and moved on.

But how did he feel? Positive thinking was all very well, but where did he go from here? He might want to help his father, but he was loath to make things too easy for his brother. Tom deserved to sweat a bit. God knew, he'd done enough sweating in his time.

And as for Grace?

The realisation that he would have to ring Miranda today and apologise for cutting their evening short gave him a momentary diversion. For the first time since their relationship started, he didn't want to ring her. Maybe he could delay it, just for a day or two, he thought, despising his cowardice. Until he'd decided exactly what he was going to do.

CHAPTER SIX

GRACE thanked the woman who had shown her round the tiny one-bedroom apartment and said she would let her know. But before she'd climbed the basement steps up to the street again, Grace was already crossing another possible address off her list. Besides which, it was in one of the poorer parts of the city and, with pubs just a stone's throw away on each corner, it was unlikely to be the quiet sanctuary she craved.

But she had to get out of Tom's house. Even if it meant moving into Newcastle itself. She had a car—albeit an old one—so she was mobile. And there was nowhere suitable in Tayford that wouldn't entail an argument with her present landlord.

All the same, she was becoming a little downhearted. On the rent she could afford, her choices were few and far between. If only Tom's mother and father were at home, she might have been able to move in with them. Mrs Ferreira, certainly, would understand her situation now that Sophie had gone back to her mother.

Climbing back into her Mini, she started the engine and drove away from Byker Avenue. There was only one other address left on her list, but she didn't have the heart to visit it today. Besides, it was already after eight and Tom would be wondering where she was. Her frequent excuses, about visiting the gym, were beginning to wear rather thin.

To her relief, Tom wasn't in when she got back. A note stuck to the fridge door informed her that he was having dinner with his bank manager and might be late. Grace was relieved—and impressed—although she suspected Tom had

initiated the hospitality. He always said you had to specu-
late to accumulate, but Grace didn't know how true that
was.

The phone rang as she was studying the contents of the
fridge, trying to decide whether she'd prefer a baked potato
topped with cheese, or a simple omelette. She didn't do
much cooking these days, something else she hoped to
change when she had her own place. Fast food was all very
well, but it couldn't compete with real home cooking.

Snatching the phone off the wall, she jammed it between
her shoulder and her ear as she took a couple of eggs and
a pack of cheddar out of the fridge. A cheese omelette
sounded appetising, and there was a head of lettuce in the
salad drawer.

'Yes,' she said, expecting it to be for Tom and preparing
to tell whoever was calling that he wasn't available. But
the phone nearly dropped onto the floor when she heard a
deep, vaguely familiar, voice say, 'Grace?'

It was Oliver Ferreira. She didn't know why she was
certain; she hardly knew the man, for heaven's sake. But
his dark attractive voice was unmistakable and she put
down the cheese and eggs and took hold of the receiver.

'Hi,' she said, hoping she sounded less agitated than she
felt. 'Um—Tom's not here, I'm afraid.'

'Is he not?' Oh, why did she get the feeling that he'd
known that all along? 'That's a shame.'

'I can leave a note for him to ring you when he gets in,'
she offered lamely, not knowing what else to say, but
Oliver demurred.

'No need,' he said. 'I'll catch him some other time.'
There was a pregnant pause, and then he added softly, 'Has
he left you all on your own?'

Grace pursed her lips. 'I wouldn't put it quite like that,'
she said, resenting his mocking tone. 'I am on my own,
yes. But that's how I like it.'

'Pity.' She heard him give what sounded like a regretful sigh, but what did she know? 'I was going to ask if you'd like to have supper with me. Providing you haven't eaten already, of course.'

Grace sucked in a breath. 'I—' The cheese and eggs lying on the counter mocked her now, but she couldn't bring herself to refuse him. Not outright, anyway. 'I haven't eaten, as it happens.'

'Does that mean you'll come?'

Grace hesitated. 'Why do you want to have supper with me, Mr Ferreira?'

'Maybe I want to explore my attraction to you,' he said drily, and Grace was overcome with embarrassment at the memory of what she'd said the last time they were together.

'I—don't think so,' she said at last and Oliver immediately took her up on it.

'You don't think what?' he queried. 'That I'm attracted to you or that you'll accept my invitation?'

Grace swallowed. 'I—both, I guess.'

'Why?'

'You know why,' she said, the cheese and eggs regaining a little of their attraction. 'But thanks for the offer.' And without waiting to say anything more, she put the receiver back on its hook.

To her annoyance, she found she was trembling, and despite her hunger she shoved the makings for the omelette back in the fridge. A sandwich would have to do, she decided, no longer in the mood to cook for herself and, pulling a plastic-wrapped loaf out of the bread bin, she started to unwind the fastener.

She'd pricked her finger on the metal insert and was sucking it frustratedly when someone rang the doorbell. Now what? she fretted, striding impatiently out of the kitchen and along the hall to the door. The only person she could think it might be was Sophie, but surely she still had her key.

Not even considering she was taking a chance by opening the door after dark when she was alone in the house, she turned the latch and pulled it open.

'*Oliver!*'

His name sprang from her lips, almost without her volition, and for a moment she could only stare at him as if she didn't quite believe her eyes. She blinked. It was barely five minutes since she'd put down the phone. How could he be here? It didn't make sense.

Yet, here he was. She had only to feel the familiar prickling of her skin to know she wasn't imagining it. In a black shirt, black jeans and a black leather jerkin, he looked vaguely foreign, but she knew it was just his Spanish blood that was showing tonight.

'You really shouldn't open the door without checking to see who it is first,' he remarked, one hand outstretched to support himself against the frame. 'Or were you expecting someone else?'

'I think that's my business, don't you?' she retorted, unconsciously aping his reply when she'd asked if he wanted a family. A faint smile touched his thin lips.

'I'll take that as a no,' he said, placing one booted foot on the lower step. 'May I come in?'

No!

Grace pressed her lips together. How could she refuse him? It wasn't her house. 'If you like,' she replied rather ungraciously and, turning on her heel, she retreated along the hall.

She knew he was following her. Although the sound of the outer door slamming might have meant anything, she was conscious of him with every fibre of her being. If only he weren't so big, so dark, so disturbingly male, she thought, despising herself for wanting him to stay. But what on earth was he doing here?

She paused in the centre of the kitchen, briefly unable to remember what she had been about to do before he rang the bell. Then she saw the loaf of bread and the fastener that had caused her so much grief and expelled a heavy sigh. A sandwich, she reminded herself firmly. She had been about to make a sandwich.

He halted in the doorway, propping his shoulder against the jamb, studying her with deeply intent dark eyes. 'What are you doing?'

Grace lifted one shoulder in a dismissive shrug. But she was wishing she were wearing something a little more alluring than a cropped tee shirt and jeans. Okay, the jeans were cut low on her hips and her tee shirt exposed tantalising glimpses of her midriff and the tiny rose tattoo that she'd had done in a weak moment and regretted ever since. But they were definitely not what she would have chosen to wear had she had a choice.

'What does it look like I'm doing?' she asked, taking a knife from the drawer. 'What do you want?'

'It looks like you're about to make yourself a sandwich,' he remarked, answering her first question but not her second. 'Should I feel insulted, I wonder? It appears you'd rather make do with a—what? A cheese sandwich?—than have supper with me.'

Grace expelled a tight breath. 'What are you doing here, Oliver? Where were you when you phoned me? In the pub?'

'I was sitting in my car at your gate,' he confessed ruefully. 'I thought I'd better phone before putting in an appearance.'

'What for?' Grace permitted herself a brief glance in his direction. 'You obviously had every intention of coming here.'

'Well—yeah.' He conceded the point. 'But I don't like being hung up on. Do you?'

Grace shook her head. 'I didn't hang up on you,' she protested. But she knew she had. 'In any case, as I said before, Tom's not here.'

'I know.' He shrugged. 'I knew that before you told me.'

So she hadn't been wrong. 'How did you know? Have you spoken to him?'

'No.' Oliver hesitated a moment and then he said, 'His bank manager is a friend of mine.'

Grace frowned. 'So you set up this meeting for him?'

'No.' Oliver sighed. 'George Green told me he was meeting Tom for dinner.'

'Why would he tell you something like that?' She stared at him. 'Aren't clients' affairs supposed to be confidential?'

Oliver made an exasperated sound. 'He didn't betray any confidences, Grace. We were both at a planning meeting this afternoon. He mentioned he was having dinner with Tom this evening.'

'So when you rang earlier, you knew perfectly well that Tom wouldn't be here?'

'Looks like it.'

Grace put down the knife, her fingers curling into her palms. 'So why did you pretend you thought he was?'

'As I recall, you told me Tom wasn't here before I could say anything,' he essayed evenly. 'I just played along.'

Grace pressed her lips together. 'So why did you ring?'

'Need you ask?' Oliver straightened away from the door. 'I wanted to see you again. On my terms, not Tom's.'

Grace's mouth felt dry and when he moved, smoothly but inexorably, towards her, she couldn't prevent her tongue from emerging to moisten her parched lips. 'I think you should go,' she said, but one of his hands had fastened around her wrist and before she had finished the words he raised it to his lips.

'You don't mean that,' he said, his tongue exploring the sensitive network of veins he'd turned towards his mouth. His teeth nipped at the thin veil of skin. 'So vulnerable,' he murmured huskily. 'Don't tell me you don't want to find out where this is going.'

Grace had the feeling she knew exactly where it was going, if she let it. This close to him, it was difficult to think of anything else, her senses assaulted by the heat of his nearness, the clean scent of his maleness. The awareness that he could overpower her so easily should have scared her, but it didn't. Yet she couldn't deny she had little resistance to his dark magnetism.

A trickle of perspiration ran down between her breasts, dampening her bra, and although she knew he couldn't possibly see it, she felt as if he could. His head was still bent over her wrist, but when she shivered in response to her thoughts he looked up. Eyes that seemed to have no trace of lightness in them searched her unguarded face, and a sensual smile softened the hard contours of his mouth.

'Are you cold?' He raised his dark eyebrows, but she could only shake her head. 'I thought not,' he said with some satisfaction, and tucked an errant strand of red-gold hair behind her ear. 'Do you still want me to go?'

Grace quivered. 'Would you? If I asked you?'

Oliver's mouth tugged down at the corners. 'No,' he said irrepressibly. 'But you haven't answered my question.'

Grace swallowed. 'What do you want from me, Oliver? If this is some ploy to make your brother jealous—'

'It's not.' His eyes darkened. 'I wouldn't be so crass.' His fingers stroked her cheek, his thumb rubbing insistently across her soft lips. 'I know you don't need me to tell you that you're beautiful, but you are, you know? So beautiful it hurts.'

Grace moved her head from side to side, dislodging his fingers from her face. 'I don't need any unnecessary compliments,' she said a little hoarsely. 'I just want to know why you're doing this?'

'Isn't it obvious?' And now his hands were on her bare midriff, urging her towards him, bringing her lower body into intimate contact with his. 'Does that tell you anything?'

Grace's legs had turned to jelly at the first touch of his hands on her body and an unfamiliar ache in the pit of her stomach made her feel weak. He parted his legs then so that she was drawn between them, the heavy pressure of his arousal unmistakable.

But almost before her brain had had time to process that thought, Oliver bent towards her, his lips brushing softly but insistently over hers. The breath she'd hardly been aware she was holding escaped on a sigh as he continued to tease her, and she swayed towards him, her breasts flattening eagerly against his hard chest.

It was so different from any kiss she'd experienced before. He wasn't forceful or urgent, but when he caught the soft flesh of her lower lip between his teeth and bit her, her bones felt as if they were melting into water.

She was hardly aware of his hands sliding over her hips to the rounded curve of her bottom. It was only when he started to caress her, when the tips of his fingers invaded the soft cleft at the top of her legs, that she sagged against him. A pulse in the moist hollow he had barely brushed against was throbbing with a powerful, sensuous beat and, as if he knew exactly how she was feeling, Oliver deepened the kiss, his mouth settling hotly and surely over hers.

Her head swam as the wet thrust of his tongue invaded her mouth. A low moan—half protest, half invitation—escaped her, the blood thundering hotly through her veins. He was seducing her with his mouth, was her last coherent thought before a mindless lethargy gripped her. He was using his tongue to imitate what he wanted to do with another part of his body, and when he rotated his hips against hers she was instantly drenched with a wet, sexual heat.

'I want you,' he said thickly, backing her up against the unit behind her. The pressure of his body on hers kept her there, his hands supporting him at either side as he continued to bestow long, drugging kisses on her lips, her cheek, the soft, yielding curve of her throat. 'I wanted you the first time I saw you. Crazy, huh?'

Grace trembled. 'I don't think it's crazy at all,' she gulped unsteadily, tipping her head to one side to make it easier for him to nuzzle her shoulder. 'I was attracted to you, too. But then, you know that.'

'Do I?' He looked down at her, watching her reaction when his hands sought the hem of her tee shirt, sliding beneath it to caress the creamy flesh that covered her ribs. His thumbs brushed the undersides of her breasts, his eyes darkening when he discovered she wasn't wearing a bra. 'I think we're wearing too many clothes.'

'So do I,' she confessed, her hands spreading against his shirt, feeling the powerful throb of his heart beneath her palms.

'We should get naked,' he murmured, his tongue making a lazy pass over the hard nipple that was clearly visible against her tee shirt, and she shivered in pleasurable anticipation. 'But not here,' he went on, resisting her efforts to remove his jacket and stepping back from her. 'Not in Tom's house.' He looked about him with sudden dislike. 'Not where he f— brings his women.'

Grace sagged against the unit. It took an effort but she managed to put her own hands on the counter beside her, supporting herself as she had done earlier. 'You—you mean Sophie,' she said, her bemused brain taking time to assimilate his words. Of course, she thought, this house would for ever be associated with his ex-wife's betrayal.

'Whatever,' he said, but before she could ask him what

he meant by that they both heard the sound of a car turning into the driveway outside.

'That's Tom,' she exclaimed, all other considerations forgotten in the sudden shock of his return. She glanced half guiltily at the clock, tugging her tee shirt back into place. 'He's early. It's only nine o'clock.'

'Maybe his meeting didn't go as well as he'd expected,' remarked Oliver, his expression hardening. 'I guess this is where I came in.'

'What do you mean?'

Grace was still staring uncomprehendingly at him when Tom's key rattled in the lock. The front door opened and slammed behind him with a definite thump. Then he was striding down the hall and, unable to stand there as Oliver was doing, pretending that nothing had happened, Grace turned away to snatch up the knife again as Tom appeared in the doorway.

His greeting to his brother was hardly friendly. 'What are you doing here?' he snapped, looking suspiciously from one to the other of them, and Grace thought that if he was still hoping to get some financial assistance from Oliver, he was hardly going the right way about it.

'Yeah, I'm pleased to see you, too,' Oliver responded drily, and Grace envied him his apparent complacency even as she resented it.

'Well…' Tom's jaw bunched, but Grace noticed that much of his anger had been defused by his brother's cool-ness. 'I've had a bloody awful evening, haven't I?'

'And finding me here hasn't improved it?' suggested Oliver evenly. 'No, well, it's not my fault that you got yourself into a mess.'

'I know that.' Tom's nostrils flared. 'You don't have to rub it in. Anyway, you still haven't told me why you're here. Have you had a change of heart?'

'You wish.' Oliver was sardonic. 'No, as a matter of fact,

I knew you were supposedly having dinner with George Green this evening and I called to ask Miss Lovell if she would care to have supper with me.' His lips twisted. 'Not unexpectedly, she declined.'

Tom's bushy eyebrows drew together in obvious surprise but Grace, meeting Oliver's enigmatic gaze, felt the sudden chill of knowing that what had happened had meant nothing to him.

'Yeah, well, Gracie's fussy about who she has supper with,' Tom declared smugly, evidently deciding that her decision must have had something to do with him. He slipped a possessive arm about her shoulders. 'Have you had a good evening, babe? Did you go to the gym?'

Grace could hardly bear to have him touch her, but any-thing was better than allowing Oliver to see how humiliated she felt. 'It's been—interesting,' she said, moving out of Tom's embrace. 'I—think I'll go and take a shower. I feel—dirty.'

'Don't go on my account,' said Oliver abruptly as she dropped the knife and made as if to leave. 'I'll see you later, Tom.' And without giving either of them the chance to detain him, he strode back along the hall to the door.

The door had hardly banged behind him before Tom turned on Grace. 'What was that all about? What's been going on here, Gracie? What did he really want?'

'He told you why he came here,' she retorted, feeling the anger of knowing she'd been used stirring again. 'And don't call me Gracie! I don't like it.'

Tom ignored that. 'He actually came to ask you out?' He snorted. 'He's got a nerve!'

'Why?' Grace was just incensed enough to argue with him. 'Why shouldn't he ask me out? I'm a free agent and so is he.'

Tom sneered. 'I wouldn't let Sophie hear you say that if I were you,' he retorted. 'She still considers Oliver her property. She always has. Even when she was with me, she was always keeping tabs on him, checking who he went out with, who he slept with.'

'I don't want to hear this,' exclaimed Grace, ignoring the way her stomach clenched when Tom spoke of Oliver sleeping with anyone else. 'I'm not going out with him, so whether Sophie would approve or otherwise is a moot point.' She swallowed. 'And now I really am going to have a shower. Okay?'

Tom hesitated. 'I'm really glad, you know,' he said, stepping into her path as she started for the door. 'That you turned Oliver down, I mean. You and me—we've got unfinished business.'

Grace's jaw dropped. 'Tom—'

'No. Don't say anything now.' He gave her an appealing little-boy look. 'This has been one hell of an evening and I don't think I could take any more rejection. Not tonight. Green turned me down, you know? He says a hundred is all I'm good for. So where the hell am I going to get the rest?'

Grace decided she couldn't take any more of this. Staying on after Sophie walked out had been a mistake and if she wasn't careful, she was going to pay for it, big time.

Perhaps if she got away for a few days, right away, she'd feel a little less trapped. Maybe Tom would realise he had to solve his own problems, too, she thought, though not so optimistically. Nevertheless, when she got back, she was definitely going to get a place of her own.

'I'm sorry,' she said now. And she was, if perhaps not for the reasons he assumed. Then, squaring her shoulders, she added, 'Look, I'm thinking of taking a few days off, actually. Dad's always asking me to spend some time with them and I know they're going to the villa at the weekend for a couple of weeks. I thought I'd go with them, if that's okay with you?'

Tom's shoulders sagged. 'I suppose I can't stop you, if that's what you want to do,' he said at last. 'But you know I'm going to miss you, don't you?'

Grace couldn't bring herself to say, 'I'll miss you, too', even though she knew he expected it. 'I'll only be away a week,' she said, despising herself for giving in to his emotional blackmail. 'Who knows? Maybe—Oliver…' She had difficulty saying his name but somehow she managed it. 'Maybe he will change his mind.'

'I won't hold my breath,' said Tom bitterly, jerking open the fridge door to take a beer from inside and Grace took the opportunity to sidestep him and reach the door. He turned then, looking after her with sad, mournful eyes. 'But you go and enjoy yourself, Gracie. You deserve it. We'll talk again when you get back.'

CHAPTER SEVEN

IT WAS the sun that woke him. Slanting through the blinds, it was so much stronger than the sun at home and the room, generous though it was, was getting uncomfortably airless.

Oliver turned over onto his back and gazed up at the ceiling above his head, briefly wondering where he was. Then comprehension dawned, and he lifted both hands to push the tangled weight of his hair off his forehead. He was in Spain, in San Luis, in his parents' spare bedroom to be precise, and for the next few days he had nothing to do but relax and chill out.

Well, that was the story anyway, he conceded, spreading his arms to push himself into a sitting position and taking a moment to survey his surroundings. Chilling out implied a sense of relaxation he was far from feeling and even escaping to Spain hadn't released him from the guilty prison of his thoughts.

Grace.

As always, her name came first to his mind. Although it was several days since he'd left her in Tom's house, he hadn't been able to get what happened out of his head. Never mind that she was untrustworthy, that she was living with one brother and yet apparently thought nothing of making out with the other. Somehow, she had bewitched him and he didn't see the situation changing any time soon.

All the same, he was ashamed of how he had behaved. Oh, not at walking out. That had probably been the most sensible thing he'd done that night. But touching her, giving in to the almost primitive emotions she aroused in him, that had been stupid. What about Miranda, for God's sake? What about Tom?

In her own way, Grace was just as bad as Sophie. Okay, she wasn't married to Tom, but it was obvious he considered her his property. Whether he was prepared to use her to gain his own ends was another matter, however. And it wasn't a situation Oliver wanted to explore.

Which was why he'd been glad to have an excuse to leave the country. He'd already entertained the idea of speaking to his father face to face about his financial problems and it had been a handy excuse to give Miranda when she'd questioned his decision to make the trip at such short notice.

'If only you'd given me some warning,' she'd exclaimed a couple of nights ago when he'd phoned her to break the news. 'I have some holiday due. I could have deferred my cases and come with you.'

Oliver had expressed his regret, of course, but in all honesty the last thing he needed right now was another woman's company. He needed space, he told himself. A time to get his head round this compulsive, but totally unwanted, desire he felt for his brother's mistress.

His parents had been touchingly glad to see him, which had only added to his sense of culpability. He hadn't visited them half often enough, neither here nor in England, in the years since he and Sophie split up, and although he'd always assured himself that Tom had always been his father's favourite, he knew in his heart of hearts that it wasn't true. George and Nancy Ferreira were equally proud of both their sons and they'd suffered terribly when the family had been torn apart.

Now, after a glance at the watch he'd left on the bedside cabinet, Oliver thrust his long legs out of bed. Then, getting to his feet, he walked across to unlatch the long windows that opened onto the wraparound veranda outside.

It was nearly half past nine, and Oliver was amazed at how well he had slept. Of course, he and his father had sat up late the previous evening, catching up on each other's news, and no doubt his mother had decided to let him sleep in. Even so, it was a while since he'd slept so soundly, and this morning he felt considerably more invigorated than he'd done the night before.

Which was just as well considering that, although they'd covered most matters, both he and his father had avoided any mention of Tom or his financial problems. Sooner or later Oliver was going to have to find out exactly what his father knew—if anything—and what he thought his older son should do.

The sound of the door opening behind him had Oliver reaching automatically for the end of the sheet to cover his nakedness. But it was only his mother who bustled into the room carrying a tray containing a pot of coffee and some warm cinnamon-scented rolls.

'Ah, you're up,' she said, setting the tray down on the bedside cabinet and regarding him with obvious pleasure. 'Did you sleep well?'

'Very well,' said Oliver, dragging the sheet off the bed and winding it around his waist. He looked ruefully at the tray. 'You didn't have to do this.'

'I know I didn't.' His mother spoke briskly. 'But it's not every day I have my elder son staying with me. I want you to feel you're always welcome here.'

Oliver felt another twinge of shame. 'I know that, Mum.'

'So long as you do.' She came towards him, reaching up to bestow a warm kiss on his jawline. 'It's been too long, Oliver.'

He nodded, touched anew by the warmth of their welcome. 'Where's Dad?'

'Oh, he's reading the morning paper,' she said, glancing about the room as she spoke. 'Now, have you got any washing you need doing? Maria comes at ten and she's never overworked.'

Oliver grinned. 'Believe it or not, Mum, but I'm quite capable of loading a washing machine for myself. Besides which, I have a very efficient housekeeper who keeps me in order.'

'I'm pleased to hear it.' Mrs Ferreira permitted herself another doubtful glance in his direction before making for the door. 'Enjoy your breakfast.

'I'm sure I will.'

His mother paused with one hand on the door. 'You are—all right, aren't you, Oliver?' Her cheeks took on a tinge of pink. 'We heard about—well, about Sophie and Tom. I expect that was quite a shock for you.'

Oliver sighed. 'A surprise, certainly,' he admitted. 'But it doesn't make any difference to me, Mum. Honestly.'

She hesitated. 'You're not thinking of taking her back, then?'

'God, no!' He was surprised how repulsive that thought was.

'Good.' She gave him a relieved smile. 'Well, then, I'll go and see what your father is doing. Don't hurry. There's nothing spoiling.'

An hour later, Oliver, dressed in shorts and a tank-top, emerged from his room to find Maria, his parents' house-maid, vacuuming the rug in the living room. She seemed genuinely pleased to see him and they exchanged a few words in her language before he went in search of his father.

It was amazing, he thought. He'd learned to speak Spanish when he was at school and during frequent holidays in Spain, and whenever he came back here it seemed the most natural thing to lapse into that language. It must be in his genes, he mused, remembering, rather reluctantly, that Tom had always had a problem with languages.

His parents were sitting on the patio, enjoying a mid-morning pot of coffee. The villa, which was set in the hills above the small village of San Luis, had a marvellous view of the ocean, and feeling the sun warm on his shoulders, Oliver allowed a sense of well-being to envelop him.

'Come and sit down,' said his mother, getting immediately to her feet. 'I'll get another cup. Do you want anything to eat?'

'Nothing, thanks.' Oliver caught her arm as she would have hurried past him and halted her progress. 'Sit down, Mum. Enjoy your coffee. I've just had breakfast, remember?'

'Well, if you're sure?'

'I am.' Oliver waited until she'd resumed her seat before perching on the low wall that surrounded the patio, taking a deep breath of the pine-scented air. All around him, evidence of his father's love of gardening was rampant, lush tropical blossoms growing side by side with roses and geraniums. Above his head, a tumble of bougainvillea defined the latticework of a bamboo pergola, and along the terrace, tubs of fuchsia and impatiens cast their own perfumes onto the breeze.

'Your mother says you had a good night,' observed George Ferreira, putting aside his newspaper and regarding his son with a dark, appraising gaze. 'I don't know why you don't come out here more often. You know you're always welcome.'

'I know.'

'I mean it.' The older man was gruff. 'And if you want to bring that young woman of yours with you, we wouldn't mind.'

Oliver nodded. 'Thanks, Dad.'

'Miranda, isn't it?' his mother queried. 'Didn't you say she's a lawyer? That must be a fascinating occupation.'

Oliver really didn't want to talk about Miranda, but he

knew his parents were just interested and he couldn't refuse to answer them.

'I expect it is,' he said now. 'She seems to like it, anyway.'

'And is it serious? Your relationship, I mean?' asked Mrs Ferreira innocently, only to have her husband impale her with a hard dark gaze.

'Leave it alone, Nancy,' he exclaimed, shifting impatiently in his chair. 'Dammit, the boy's only known her a couple of months. After that business with you-know-who, I'd be very wary of committing myself again and I guess he is, too.'

'Oh, George,' began his wife, taking umbrage, and Oliver, who had been amused at being called a boy again, broke in soothingly.

'We're friends, Mum. That's all,' he said, wondering how Miranda would react if she could hear him dismissing their affair so casually. He pressed down on the wall with his hands and got to his feet again. 'You know, I think I'll take a walk down to the beach.'

'To the beach?' His mother looked disapproving now. 'Oh, Oliver, it's almost a mile to the beach and you're not used to this heat.'

'For God's sake!' Mr Ferreira couldn't hide his impatience. 'Oliver's a grown man, Nancy. Stop clucking around him like an old hen! Here.' He picked a baseball cap up from the table and tossed it at his son. 'Keep her happy, son. I've got a handful of the things.'

Oliver grinned. 'Thanks,' he said, and with a reassuring smile for his mother, he vaulted over the low stone wall that edged the property and sauntered along the lane to the narrow road that led down into the village of San Luis.

The path he took also circled the villa next door to the Ferreiras'. Was this the one Grace's parents owned? he wondered, casting a swift glance towards the sprawling dwelling that was partially hidden behind a belt of greenery. The blinds were drawn, he noticed, envying them the swimming pool that glinted through a clump of palm and cypress trees. It was obviously a bigger villa than the one his parents occupied and, judging by the sprinkler spinning over the manicured lawn, Mr Lovell employed a gardener to keep his grounds in mint condition.

The sun was hot, as his mother had said, and Oliver was quite glad to pull the baseball cap onto his head. But it was the back of his neck that needed protection, and he wore it back to front, feeling more and more like a tourist by the time he reached the village.

Not that San Luis catered much for its foreign visitors. It was basically a fishing community, and although several expensive yachts were moored in the harbour, there were no tapas bars or high-rise hotels.

Oliver spent a little time down at the quayside, watching a couple of men, obviously father and son, loading their catch onto the back of a pick-up. He saw langoustines and other shellfish, squirming frantically in boxes of ice, and pitied the poor creatures their fate. He guessed they were bound for one of the resort hotels along the coast where scallops fried in garlic butter were a gourmet speciality.

Beyond the harbour wall, grass-studded dunes gave onto a stretch of golden sand and Oliver kicked off his loafers, tying the laces together and looping them about his neck. God, he needed this, he thought, not realising until now how long the winter had seemed. It seemed years, not months, since he and Miranda had spent ten days in Barbados in December.

He grimaced, remembering. They'd only known one another for a few weeks at that time and when he'd suggested she might like to join him on a Caribbean holiday, he'd half expected her to refuse. But she hadn't. She'd been almost pathetically eager to go with him, and he supposed their relationship had been defined from that date.

Until then, it had been a fairly open affair, with Oliver feeling free to go out with other women if he chose. After Barbados, however, Miranda had seemed to expect a certain exclusivity from him, and until he'd met Grace Lovell he'd had no real problem with that.

Which was equally pathetic, he thought, treading onto the damp sand that edged the ebbing tide. His father was right. He should have learned his lesson with Sophie. And he had, he assured himself grimly. His association with Miranda proved it. Their relationship was civilised and sexually satisfying, but at no time were his emotions involved. And that was the way he liked it.

Despite the warmth of the sun, the water was cool on his bare soles, and putting the disagreeable aspects of his thoughts aside, he started off along the beach. He hadn't come here to stress about Grace or his affair with Miranda. He'd come to talk to his father, and during the next few days he was going to have to find a way to persuade the old man to let him help him out.

Grace came out onto the sundeck at the back of the villa. She was carrying the cup of coffee she'd just made for herself in the terracotta-tiled luxury of her parents' kitchen and for a moment the brilliance of the sun dazzled her.

Her feet were bare and the thin wrapper she'd pulled on over the cotton tank-top and boxers she used to sleep in was loose. One end of the belt trailed on the ground as she sought the shade offered by the green-striped umbrella that arced over a glass-topped wicker table and chairs. Coiling one bare leg beneath her, she subsided into one of the chairs. Cupping the coffee between her palms she surveyed the view before her with real pleasure.

She'd forgotten the sea could be so blue, she thought,

the sails of a single yacht stark against that azure backdrop. Forgotten how much less complicated things could seem here, far from the people and places that made up her everyday life. She wouldn't want to live here. She was no lotus-eater. But a few days spent in these surroundings were exactly what she needed.

She'd lied when she'd told Tom that her parents had invited her. But it had only been a white lie. Her mother and father were always telling her she should take advantage of the villa whether they were there or not.

They were a fairly modern couple and they wouldn't have objected if she'd invited a young man to share the villa with her. The fact that so far Grace hadn't done so was, she knew, a source of some regret to them, but they seldom voiced it. All the same, Grace guessed they were losing hope that she would ever find a man she could love.

How would they feel if they found out that, apart from one clumsy experience when she was in her teens, Grace had never been to bed with a man? she wondered. It was not something she was proud of, not something she would have chosen for herself. But she'd learned early on that most men only saw her as a sex object. A couple of dates, if she was lucky, and then the expectation of getting into her pants.

Perhaps she'd just not met the right man yet, she thought ruefully. Or maybe she had a seriously low sex drive and that was why she found it so easy to refuse. An image of Oliver Ferreira's face when he'd walked out of Tom's kitchen that night caused an untimely shiver to feather her spine. The chilling lack of warmth in his expression, the bitter irony in the words he had exchanged with his brother, had torn her apart. Somehow he'd breached the wall she'd so carefully erected around her emotions and then tramped roughshod over the feelings he'd found inside.

But she didn't want to think about Oliver, she reminded

herself, getting up from the table again and drifting aimlessly down the shallow steps that led to the pool. She took another sip of her cooling coffee and stiffened her spine. She'd come away to avoid thinking of him and she wasn't going to do herself any good at all if she spent all her time fretting over him. It was ridiculous. He was no better than any of the other men who'd attempted to make love to her. He'd been just as keen to get her clothes off.

The difference was, she'd been just as keen to help him, she acknowledged wryly. Remembering his hands on her body, his thumbs brushing her breasts, his tongue laving a hot path down her throat, she shivered anew. Oh, God, she'd never known what it was like to want a man until he'd touched her, and now she found it incredibly hard to think of anything else.

Sighing, she set the coffee cup down on a low table beside a cushioned lounger and, stepping nearer to the edge of the pool, she dipped a tentative toe in the water.

It was cool, but she'd expected that. Until the sun gained its full strength, the pool was never as warm as the sea. Lifting her head, she looked towards the vast expanse of blue that stretched towards the horizon and sighed again. It was all so beautiful, so peaceful. Why couldn't she just relax and enjoy it?

She had lifted her cup and was just about to walk back towards the house when she saw a man turn into the narrow lane that ran along the back of the property. From a distance, all she could really see was that he was tall and dark but, as the lane connected with several properties in the area, she wasn't surprised to see someone using it as a short cut. He could be a Spaniard, she thought. He was certainly dark enough, and she wondered if someone new had moved into one of the villas.

But as he drew nearer a paralysing numbness kept her rooted to the spot. He was no Spaniard—well, only half, anyway, and that half diluted by years of living in a colder climate. Was that what made him so cool, so controlled? Or had Sophie bled every drop of human emotion from him?

Fortunately, there was a barrier of trees between her and the lane. It wasn't wholly successful as a screen, but it did offer her some protection, and if she slipped away now he need never know she was here.

But even as she attempted to move, to force some strength into limbs that felt oddly alien to her, he turned his head and saw her. She saw the recognition dawn in his eyes, saw his momentary confusion when he realised she had seen him, too, and wanted to die of shame.

Then, instead of ignoring her as she'd half expected, he crossed to the fence that edged the property and vaulted over it. Pushing aside the scale-like leaves of a spreading conifer, he stepped onto the lawn and said in a low, disturbing drawl, 'Well, well. Grace! This is an unexpected pleasure.'

CHAPTER EIGHT

HE WAS a liar, she thought, resenting the way her pulse raced every time he looked at her. She'd never seen a man who looked so good in shorts before, and his navy tank-top only accentuated the dark tan of his skin.

His feet, like hers, were bare, his legs and his forearms lightly covered with hair. His skin had a sheen to it and she assumed he'd been sweating on the walk up from the village. For that was where she guessed he'd been. He had probably been on the beach, too.

But although she'd never found a sweating man appealing in the past, everything about Oliver Ferreira attracted her. She had to drag her gaze from his lean, disturbing face before he saw something in hers that she didn't want him to see.

To her relief, she found her limbs would move now and, gathering the ends of her belt about her, she turned back to the steps that led up to the terrace. 'I didn't know you were planning on coming out here,' she said half defensively. 'Did Tom tell you I was here?'

'Yeah, right.' Oliver was sardonic. 'Believe it or not, I haven't spoken to my brother in days.'

In four days to be precise, she guessed unwillingly, but that was definitely not a topic for discussion. 'Oh, well,' she said instead. 'I got the impression from your mother that you never came here.'

'Or you wouldn't have?' he suggested drily, coming to stand at the top of the steps so that Grace abruptly changed her mind about climbing them. 'I could say I didn't know you were planning a holiday either.'

'I wasn't.' Her response was far too revealing, however, and unwilling to give him the impression that he had had anything to do with her decision, she added swiftly, 'But my mother and father are always urging me to take advantage of this place.'

'Your mother and father are here?'

'I—not—not yet,' she stumbled awkwardly. 'But they're planning on taking a break in a couple of weeks.'

And why had she had to tell him that? she chided herself irritably. He would think she wanted him to know she was on her own. And she didn't. *She didn't.*

Oliver absorbed this in silence and then, to her dismay, he came down the steps towards her. He moved easily, lithely, his limbs moving in perfect harmony with one another, the denim of his shorts alternately tightening then loosening across his powerful thighs.

But his eyes were on the pool now, thank goodness, and hoping it didn't look too obvious, Grace eased away to where a couple of cushioned lounge chairs offered her some protection.

'When did you get here?' he asked, just as she had been beginning to hope that topic had been dealt with, and she blew out a nervous breath.

'Um...' There was no avoiding that one and Grace gave in. 'I just got here last night, actually,' she said, trying to remember whether Tom had spoken to his brother since her decision. 'How—how about you?'

'A couple of days ago,' he answered, approaching the edge of the pool and dipping his toe as she had done earlier. 'But you're right. I'm not a regular visitor.'

'Oh.'

Grace nodded, trying not to notice that his tank-top left a wedge of smooth brown skin visible when he bent towards the water. His shorts slipped low on his hips and she found herself wondering if his was an all-over tan. It certainly looked that way.

Then she realised he had straightened and turned back to her and she hurriedly directed her attention elsewhere. Dear Lord, she didn't know what was the matter with her. She'd never found herself speculating about a man's body before.

But then, she'd never remembered every second she'd spent with a man before. Yet she could recall every moment of their encounter at Tom's house in intimate detail. She'd wanted to be close to him, wanted to feel his hands on her body, wanted to give herself to him in a way that had terrified her by its intensity.

But it hadn't happened then, and it wasn't going to happen now, she assured herself. Even if she was so lacking in self-respect that she was prepared to forgive him for the way he had treated her, Oliver was unlikely to change his mind about her.

And who could blame him? she mused bitterly. Tom had done everything he could to give him the impression that they were having an affair, and short of saying, 'Hey, Oliver, I'm not sleeping with Tom, you know?' her hands were tied.

In any case, did it really matter? Just because Oliver had kissed her she was imagining them having some meaningful relationship, when the possibility was that he had only been using her to bait his brother.

'Pool's cold,' he said now, stepping away from the rim. 'Do you use it?'

'Sometimes.' Grace tried to sound casual. 'You're welcome to use it, too, if you want to.'

Now why had she said that? Grace stifled a groan as Oliver's eyebrows arched in surprise.

'You wouldn't mind?'

'Why should I?' That was sufficiently indifferent, wasn't it? 'It's not my pool.'

Oliver's mouth compressed. 'Right.'

'I mean it.' She straightened her spine. 'But now I must go and get dressed.'

'Why?'

'Why?' She hoped she sounded less shocked than she felt.

'Yeah, why?' He took steps that brought him nearer to her. 'Don't get dressed on my account.' His eyes darkened. 'I like you the way you are.'

Grace's breathing quickened, but the memory of how he'd abandoned her when his brother arrived the other night stiffened her resolve.

'You're very kind,' she said tightly. 'But I know you don't mean it.'

'I do.' He came closer so that now only the width of one of the lounge chairs separated them. 'I do mean it. Why would you think I didn't?'

Grace gasped. 'Why would I think that?' she countered. 'Oh, well, let me see, could it have anything to do with the fact that you couldn't wait to get away from me the night you came to Tom's house?'

Oliver's dark features hardened. 'Do you blame me?' He hooked his thumbs into the hip pockets of his shorts. 'I prefer not to do my lovemaking with an audience. Or would you like me to have had sex with you in front of him? Forgive me, but I don't think that was a goer, do you?'

'You flatter yourself,' she exclaimed hotly. 'What makes you think I wanted to have sex with you under any circumstances?'

'You didn't?' Ignoring her attempt to hang onto the back of the lounger, he jerked the chair aside so that she dropped the ends of her belt onto the ground again. Then he moved closer, studying her tense face with a lazy sensuous gaze.

'I think you did,' he said, bending to capture the errant cord and using it to pull her towards him. 'Women like to tease,' he added, his warm breath fanning her cheek. 'Were you trying to make Tom jealous? 'Cos here's a newsflash. You succeeded.'

'I wasn't trying to make anybody jealous,' she retorted a little breathlessly, overwhelmingly conscious of his bare leg brushing her thigh. 'I didn't invite you to come to the house that night. You did that all by yourself.'

'So I did.' He looked down at her intently, his eyes lingering almost tangibly on her mouth. He was making it impossible for her to breathe normally, his behaviour projecting the same raw sensuality he had exhibited that night.

'I ought to get dressed,' she said again, wishing he would stop staring at her. Even in fraying denim shorts and a tank-top, he was in control. She, on the other hand, wasn't. Her thin cotton top and the baggy boxers were hardly flattering and her robe was slipping off one shoulder. In addition to which, she was fairly sure her braid had broken free of its fastening in her sleep and was now spilling hair down around her shoulders.

'Why don't we go for a swim instead?' he suggested huskily, tipping the robe off her other shoulder so that it fell to the ground at her feet. 'You're not wearing anything under that outfit, which is convenient, and I don't like to swim alone.'

Grace was dismayed at the way her body reacted to that invitation but she had no intention of letting him know it. 'I'm sure you never have to do anything alone,' she declared, backing away again now that she was free of the robe. 'But contrary to the opinion you obviously have of me, I don't go skinny-dipping with anyone.'

'Why not?' He came after her, fisting a handful of her top and using it to prevent her from retreating any further. 'Surely you're not a prude? Not with a body that was made to be seen and admired. Even the little rose tattoo.' His eyes darkened, dropping down over her in a way that caused her skin to grow even hotter than it already was. 'Show it to me again.'

She swallowed, intensely aware of his knuckles digging through the cloth, hard against her stomach. 'Show you what again?'

But she knew what he meant, and remembering where the rose tattoo was situated, she was surprised it wasn't already burning his fingers.

'Take this top off and we'll both be able to see,' he countered, and she was shocked to feel his hand cupping the back of her thigh just beneath the hem of the boxers. 'And these,' he added. 'You know you want to.'

'I don't.'

But she did. Just the touch of those long, cool fingers against her flesh and she was alive to every palpitating nerve in her leg, aware of her own arousal in the wet heat that was pulsing between her thighs.

'I don't believe you,' he retorted, bending towards her, his tongue tracing the dryness of her parted lips. 'You want this every bit as much as I do. The other night—' he shrugged '—it was all wrong. Wrong time, wrong place.' He released her top and circled the nape of her neck with his free hand, his thumb nudging the sensory hollow beneath her ear. Then his mouth brushed hers in a kiss that was no less disquieting because it was feather-light. 'This is right. This is good. And we're not likely to be disturbed.'

Grace raised one hand to his chest, trying, not very successfully, to hold him back. 'How—how do you know that?'

He looked surprised. 'You said your parents weren't here,' he reminded her.

'They're not. But that doesn't mean I'm alone,' she insisted, knowing how he would interpret that, and breathed a little more easily when he lifted both hands to her face.

'So who is it?' he asked, his thumbs stroking the hectic splash of colour that darkened her cheeks. 'Not Tom?'

'No, not Tom,' she retorted a little crossly, resisting the urge she had to slip her hand beneath his vest and explore the taut muscles she could feel through the fabric. 'He's not the only friend I have.'

'Oh, I believe you,' he mocked, and his tone did nothing to assuage her resentment towards him. 'But something tells me you're just whistling in the dark.' His fingers threaded through the red-gold hair that was escaping in soft tendrils about her ears. 'What are you afraid of, Gracie? That you might actually like it if you let yourself go?'

Her teeth ground together, half in anger, half in frustration. 'Don't—don't call me Gracie,' she commanded angrily, both hands holding him off now. 'It's not my name.'

'It's what Tom calls you.'

'And he knows I hate it, too.'

'Okay.' Faint amusement tugged at the corners of his mouth. 'What would you like me to call you? Sweetheart? Darling? *Baby?*'

'Grace will do,' she declared stiffly, even as his lips trailing sensually over the shoulder he had bared by pushing the shoulder of her tank-top aside caused her to shiver involuntarily. 'Oliver, please…'

'I try to,' he murmured, deliberately misunderstanding her. His hands slid from her shoulders to the curve of her back and almost instinctively she arched against him. 'Mmm, that's nice.' His fingers probed the waistband of her boxers, slipping inside to touch her bare bottom. 'Very nice.'

She wanted to stop him. She wanted to tell him that, no matter how experienced he thought she was, she was not the free spirit he believed her to be. And with anyone else, it would have been easy. It had been easy enough in the past to avoid awkward situations, but then, she'd always been in control. Now she wasn't. Now her own body was betraying her, and there seemed to be very little she could do about it.

And even as she struggled to find words to tell him he was wrong about her, his mouth claimed hers in a kiss that was neither feather-light nor controlled. The instantaneous heat that flared between them prevented that, the contact deepening instantly into a sensual assault that weakened her knees and left her helpless and clinging to him.

She heard him groan deep in his throat, as if even he had not expected such a shattering level of intimacy, and silently echoed his lament. She was very much afraid that if he hadn't been cupping her bottom, she'd have melted onto the ground at his feet.

As it was, she was conscious of every movement he made: his tongue plunging possessively into her mouth, his chest flattening her breasts, his bare legs brushing hers, his erection hard against her stomach. He couldn't hide the primitive need he was feeling any more than she could, and it was some small measure of compensation for the devastating effect he was having on her emotions.

'Hell, Grace,' he muttered, drawing back to rest his forehead against hers. 'Do you have any idea what I want to do to you?'

She could imagine. And, amazingly, it didn't scare her as it should. Indeed, right at this moment, she could think of nothing she wanted more than to let him have his way with her, and she didn't know what she'd have said if he hadn't chosen that moment to lower his head to her breast.

Her nipples were hard and swollen, their distended peaks clearly visible through the thin cloth of her top, and when he sucked one into his mouth she felt a surge of sexual need that swept clear down to her toes. Even the cloth was no barrier to the sensual tug of his teeth, and the whimper she gave betrayed her surrender.

She clutched the waistband of his shorts, loving the texture of the skin that covered his hips smooth against her knuckles. She wanted to slip her hands inside his shorts as he had done, but she wasn't that daring. Instead, she contented herself with lifting one bare foot to stroke the back of his calf, feeling his reaction in the convulsive thrust of his body.

'You were going to tell me what you wanted to do,' she reminded him in a strangled voice as he peeled the tanktop aside and took her already damp nipple into his mouth again. She caught her breath as waves of raw sensation washed over her. Then, in an effort to show that she could still think for herself, she whispered, 'I think we ought to get out of the sun.'

Oliver took a shuddering breath and she guessed he wasn't finding it easy to think coherently either. His lips gentled, softened, drew back from her breast with a lingering reluctance that she shared as much as he. 'Get out of the sun?' he echoed huskily, and as if he couldn't prevent himself, his hand moved to her breast in place of his lips, his thumb and forefinger tugging almost painfully on its swollen peak. 'Is that what you want?'

Grace sucked in a gulp of air. 'This—this is too public,' she murmured awkwardly. 'You—you saw me through the trees. Someone else could do the same.'

'Yeah, right.' Oliver heaved a sigh and with an obvious effort, his hands moved to her hips and propelled her away from him. He shook his head then, his confusion evident 'I must be crazy. You—drive me crazy. I don't know what I was thinking about.'

Grace gazed up at him anxiously. 'I thought—I hoped you were thinking about me.'

'I was.' But Oliver didn't look particularly proud to ad

mit it. His hands dropped to his sides. 'But you were right to stop me.' He stepped back, his tone flat when he spoke again. 'Thanks.'

Grace blinked. 'I didn't say I wanted you to stop,' she protested. 'I said—'

'I know what you said and I'm grateful,' Oliver retorted quickly. 'And I'm not denying any of this. But—it should not have happened.'

'Why not?' She felt indignant now, uncertain of his meaning and desperate to justify herself. 'We're—we're two adults, aren't we? Why shouldn't we—?'

'Because I'm not free,' he said harshly, and Grace's jaw dropped in disbelief.

'But, I thought you and Sophie—'

'Not Sophie,' he muttered grimly. 'There's—someone else. Someone I've been seeing for quite some time. I'm sorry.'

Grace stared at him. 'Then why did you—?'

'I've told you why,' he exclaimed bitterly. 'You make me crazy.'

'And did I make you crazy the night you came to Tom's house?' Grace asked coldly.

Oliver made a dismissive gesture. 'I suppose you must have. I'm not proud of myself.'

'You and me both,' Grace choked, humiliation closing her throat. 'Oh—go, will you? Just go. You make me sick.'

'Grace—'

'Get out of here,' she commanded and, turning on her heel, she marched up the steps and into the house.

CHAPTER NINE

IT WAS the following morning that Oliver's mother mentioned that Grace was staying at her parents' villa next door.

'You've met her, haven't you, Oliver?' she asked, busying herself with the salad she was preparing for lunch. Thankfully, she wasn't looking at him as she spoke and Oliver, who had just stopped in at the kitchen to ask where his father was, wished he hadn't bothered.

But his mother was expecting an answer, and despite his reluctance to discuss their neighbour, he had to admit that he had.

'I was sure you must have done,' Mrs Ferreira said happily, at least reassuring him that Grace had not discussed the previous morning's events with her. 'That was why I thought it would be a good idea to have her over for dinner. She's joining us this evening. She's on her own, you see. Her parents are still in England.'

Yeah, right.

Oliver expelled a heavy breath, wondering how the hell he could get out of this. After the way he'd behaved the day before, he was amazed that Grace had accepted his mother's invitation. But then, like him, she would have had a difficult time thinking of an excuse.

'She's such a nice girl, you know?' Mrs Ferreira continued, slicing an avocado into a bowl. 'Your father and I have known the Lovells for a few years now. We used to wonder if she and Tom might hit it off. But then—' Her face flushed as she realised what she was about to say, but, having committed herself, she had to go on. 'He should never have got involved with Sophie. Stupid boy!'

Oliver was relieved that his mother was so embarrassed over what she'd said that she didn't notice his response. 'There's always hope,' he said lightly, and then nodded towards the avocado. 'That looks good. Can I have a taste?'

Mrs Ferreira pretended to look disapproving, but she laid a slice of avocado on the end of her knife and offered it to him anyway. 'You don't mind, do you, Oliver?' she asked as he put the moist fruit into his mouth. 'My asking Grace to join us, I mean? As Miranda's not here, I thought you might be glad of the company.'

Oliver sighed. 'I came here to see you two. No one else,' he declared, wishing she'd asked him that before she'd made the arrangement. 'But—no. I don't mind.' He managed a thin smile, and then asked offhandedly, 'What did Grace say when you suggested it?'

'Oh, well, she said she didn't want to intrude, of course. But I explained that you wouldn't think it was intruding. That you probably missed *young* female company anyway.'

Oh, great!

Somehow Oliver managed not to let his chagrin show and, after learning that his father was sitting on the patio, he left her making the salad dressing.

But he didn't immediately go outside. For some reason— a reason that wasn't hard to fathom—he felt as if he needed a little time to himself before he spoke to anyone else. Going into his room, he flopped down on the bed. Then, resting his elbows on his knees, he buried his face in his hands.

God Almighty, he thought, what was he going to find to say to Grace? How on earth was he supposed to spend an evening in her company without betraying the effect she had on him? He could tell himself until he was blue in the face that she wasn't worth all this soul-searching, that he could control whatever it was he felt for her, but it didn't seem to work. However objectively he tried to look at it, when he was with her he thought with his sex, not his brain.

Flinging himself backwards on the bed, he stared broodingly at the ceiling. For pity's sake, he scowled savagely, what the hell was the matter with him? He wasn't an animal, dammit. He didn't waste time with women he didn't respect, and he had no respect for Grace Lovell and the game she'd initiated, playing him and Tom off against one another.

The trouble was, she looked so damn innocent, he acknowledged angrily. Until he'd seen her and Tom together, he would never have believed she was no better than his ex-wife.

All the same, it hadn't kept him away from her. He didn't know what he'd intended the night he'd gone to Tom's house and found her alone, but there was no doubt in his mind that it had included hot sex and cool sheets. He'd wanted her then and he'd wanted her yesterday morning, and if she hadn't suggested an alternative venue he might well have been reckless enough to go all the way there and then.

As it was, her words had awakened the cool voice of reason inside him, and somehow—not easily, he had to admit—he'd found the strength to get out of there. He wasn't proud that he'd had to use Miranda as an excuse, and in all honesty she did deserve better, unlike someone else he could mention.

His scowl deepened and he raked a frustrated hand through his damp hair. He'd had a shower earlier, and until his mother had exploded her bombshell, he'd been looking forward to spending the day trying to get a handle on his father's financial situation. He'd come up with a solution that he hoped might serve the dual purpose of keeping the villa and rescuing the garden centre. It meant bailing Tom out as well, but anything was better than knowing the old man was having to sell this place and spend his winters in a soulless tower block.

Now all he could think about was tonight and Grace's visit. It didn't help at all to know that she was probably dreading it just as much as he was. His mother's well-meaning plans had put him in an impossible position, and if it wouldn't have made him look like a complete coward he'd have feigned illness and cried off.

By late afternoon, Oliver had managed to convince himself that he was exaggerating the situation. What could happen, after all? It was only dinner. His father and mother would do most of the talking, and surely he could maintain a polite façade for one evening? After all, until his libido had made such a God-awful fool of itself, he'd enjoyed talking to her. She was smart and intelligent, and she obviously liked and respected his parents. Go figure.

His mother had told him that she'd asked Grace to arrive no later than seven-thirty, with dinner planned for eight o'clock, and by a quarter past the hour Oliver was pacing the patio, his second beer of the evening in his hand. Mrs Ferreira hadn't hidden her disapproval when he'd returned to the fridge for the second bottle, but he'd merely arched an inquiring brow and she'd said nothing.

Nevertheless, he knew she was worried about him, and he guessed she still suspected he harboured some feelings for his ex-wife and had come here to deal with them. If only. Oliver shook his head. Right now, Sophie and her problems were far away from his thoughts.

He stared out into the velvet darkness, feeling the soft breeze like a gentle hand against his hot skin. There were lamps on tall stalks set around the patio, but much of the garden was in shadow, a hidden source of a dozen different perfumes. From inside the villa, the familiar fragrance of his mother's tarragon sauce scented the air. She was preparing roast breasts of chicken, stuffed with a *foie gras* mousse, and his favourite pudding: a luscious custard dessert flavoured with caramel.

He was taking a mouthful of beer when he became aware that he was no longer alone. He didn't know how he knew it exactly. He'd heard nothing beyond the nightly droning of the insects. Yet he could feel eyes upon him, her eyes, and he was hardly surprised when she moved into the light

What did surprise him was the way she looked. Until then, apart from the night gear she'd been wearing the day before, he'd never seen her in anything but trousers, and it was quite a shock to see her in a skirt. And what a skirt It was a thin silk sheath in shades of bronze and black which, despite the fact that it was slit from the hem almost to her waist, still managed to cling to every curve of hip and thigh. An amber-silk sequinned halter-top completed her outfit, exposing slim arms and wrists circled by at least half a dozen thin gold bangles. The creamy slopes of her breasts displayed a tantalising cleavage, touched here and there by the red-gold glory of her hair that was loose tonight about her shoulders. Huge gold hoops, to match the bangles, hung from her ears, playing hide-and-seek among the silken strands.

But it was the supple skin of her midriff revealed as she moved that drew Oliver's eyes. A ruby jewel nestled in her navel, undulating sensually as she walked.

He'd been hot before, but now he felt a wave of raw lust dampen his skin. She was sex on legs, and he wouldn't have been human if he hadn't responded to her deliberate appeal.

Feeling as if he could drink a dozen beers and still not assuage his sudden thirst, Oliver leaned back against the wall behind him and attempted a casual greeting. 'Hi,' he said, arms crossed over his midriff, the beer bottle still in his hand. 'You look—' Incredible? Gorgeous? *Ravishing?* '—different.'

It was a lame excuse for a compliment and Grace's glossy lips twisted in a mocking smile. 'I've got my clothes on, you mean?' she offered, glancing about her as if to ensure that they were alone. 'I don't imagine you like this situation any better than I do.'

That was straight enough and Oliver restrained a wince. 'That you've got your clothes on tonight?' he responded, desperate to regain the advantage. He waited a beat. 'I gather you haven't forgiven me.'

'Forgiven you?' She halted a few feet from him, one finger toying with the gold hoop in her ear. 'For what? Leading me on? Letting me think you were interested in me? Nearly seducing me in full view of the neighbours?'

Oliver's mouth compressed and he turned to set his beer bottle down on the wall beside him. 'All of the above,' he said ruefully, surrendering to the inevitable. 'Like I said before, it shouldn't have happened.'

But who was he kidding? Not her, he guessed. He'd wanted it to happen, and she knew it. He didn't want to be attracted to her, he didn't want to feel this instant hunger every time he saw her. But he did; *he did*. So get over it, Ferreira. She's not for you.

'Don't beat yourself up over it,' she murmured now, and to his great astonishment she moved closer. 'What are you drinking?' she asked, reaching for his beer. 'Something alcoholic? I thought you didn't imbibe.'

'I don't. Usually.' Oliver attempted to take the bottle back. 'Hey, I've been drinking from that.'

'I know,' she said huskily, raising the bottle to her lips and taking a deliberate swallow. 'I can taste you on the glass.'

Oliver didn't know what he'd have done next if his father hadn't come out onto the patio at that moment. 'Oh, Grace, my dear,' he exclaimed, noticing that their visitor was standing beside his son. 'I hope Oliver's looking after you. What's that you're drinking? Beer? Oh, I'm sure we can do better than that.'

'I like beer,' Grace replied, going to meet the older man and allowing him to bestow a kiss on each cheek in turn. 'Very continental,' she teased, glancing back over her shoulder at Oliver. 'It's good to see you again, Mr Ferreira. You're looking well.'

'And you look beautiful,' exclaimed the old man warmly, blossoming under her praise. Oliver, watching them, felt a ridiculous twinge of envy. He wanted to move forward, put a possessive hand about her bare waist, make her as aware of him as he was painfully aware of her. But, of course, he couldn't.

'What, in this old thing?' she was saying now, dismissing the sequinned top and clinging skirt with a careless flick of her hand. 'Actually, I think the skirt's my mother's. It's a little tight for me.'

'In all the right places,' declared Oliver's father admiringly, and Oliver, who had never seen his father like this before, wanted to stretch out his hand and yank the old man away from her. What the hell was he doing? Didn't he know she was no better than Sophie? Why was he treating her as if butter wouldn't melt in her mouth? It made Oliver feel physically sick.

It was a great relief when his mother appeared at the French doors, her eyes taking in the scene on the patio in one all-encompassing glance.

But, although Oliver half expected her to show some impatience with his father, her smile was warm and genuine. 'Grace,' she said, stepping outside to join them. 'I hope my husband isn't embarrassing you.'

'As if he could,' retorted Grace warmly, giving the older woman a hug. 'He's an old flatterer, that's all.'

'An old something anyway,' murmured Nancy Ferreira drily. Then, turning to her husband, 'George, go and fetch the tray, will you? I think we'd all like a cocktail before dinner, hmm?'

'At your command,' agreed her husband gallantly, saluting and heading into the villa again, and Oliver's mother and Grace exchanged a mischievous look.

It made Oliver feel as if he was the outsider here and he didn't like it. His parents had never treated Sophie so affectionately, but then Sophie had never made any attempt to befriend her in-laws. Apart from Tom, that was, and he knew only too well how that had turned out.

But his mother hadn't forgotten about him, and presently she turned back, beckoning him to join them. 'Come and rescue Grace from your father, Oliver,' she exclaimed. 'She's too polite to tell him he's too old to play the fool.'

'It's my pleasure,' he said, needing no second bidding, uncaring that Grace was staring at him with wide, frustrated eyes. Then, deftly, he whipped the beer bottle out of her hand. 'Here's Dad with the cocktails. You'll have a Margarita, won't you, Grace?'

Her lips tightened for a moment and he half expected her to say something scornful in response. But courtesy— to his parents, he assumed—won out, and turning back to his father, she said, 'I'd love one. Thanks, Mr Ferreira. This is just what I need.'

They all helped themselves to a stemmed glass and then, to his embarrassment, his father decided to make a toast. 'To Oliver,' he said, raising his glass towards him. 'It's good to have you here, son. Now that—well, now that you-know-who is out of the picture, I hope we're going to see a lot more of you, business notwithstanding.'

'Hear, hear,' said Mrs Ferreira, linking her arm with Oliver's and resting her head on his shoulder for a moment.

'We've missed you, my dear. And despite his faults, I know Tom's missed you, too.'

Has he? Oliver had the feeling that all Tom had missed was his financial support. But perhaps he was being too cynical. Whatever, so long as his brother was sleeping with Grace, he doubted they could ever resume their friendship.

But he had to say something, and raising his own glass, he said, 'I'm glad to be here. I'd forgotten what it's like to be pampered.' He grimaced. 'You always make me feel so welcome. I do appreciate it.'

'Nonsense,' exclaimed his mother, but she brushed rather surreptitiously at the corner of one eye as she spoke. 'This is your home, Oliver. Just as much as that loft in Newcastle. You're welcome here at any time.'

The meal was everything his mother had hoped it would be. A spicy fish soup was followed by the tender chicken breasts, and the caramel-flavoured custard was, as Grace so aptly put it, 'To die for!'

'You can thank Oliver for that,' declared Mrs Ferreira, unknowingly eliciting another sardonic glance in his direction from their guest. 'It's his favourite. I made it especially for him.'

'How sweet!'

Grace managed not to sound as if she was being sarcastic, but Oliver knew better. If she could have taken back the compliment, she would have done so. But she couldn't. So live with it, he muttered to himself savagely, resenting the implication that he was the prodigal son.

They had coffee on the patio, the warm night air such a difference from the coolness back home. But Oliver was restless. He was finding it increasingly difficult to behave as if he and Grace were just casual acquaintances and it didn't help that she seemed to take every opportunity to provoke him.

'Do you spend a lot of time in Spain, Oliver?' she asked

with apparent innocence, and he met her cool green gaze with wary eyes.

'Unfortunately, I don't often have the chance to get away,' he replied evenly, hoping that would be an end of this particular topic, but his mother chimed in as usual.

'That's what he's always said,' she declared, eyeing her son reprovingly. 'But we're hoping that's going to change in the future.'

'Oh?' Grace arched an inquiring brow. 'May I ask why?'

No, you may not, Oliver thought grimly, suspicious of where this was leading, but his mother saw no such pitfall.

'Now that Sophie's out of the picture,' she confided, causing her son to grit his teeth. 'I'm sure you don't need me to tell you the trouble that woman's caused in this family.'

'I don't think Grace needs to hear this,' Oliver protested now with some asperity, but Mrs Ferreira only cast him a defensive look.

'Why not? It's no secret,' she declared. 'And Grace isn't likely to go gossiping about it to all and sundry.'

'Of course not.' Grace was quick to reassure them, but Oliver didn't trust her benign expression. 'I'm sure you must all be very relieved that he's found someone else.'

Ah! Oliver's lips tightened in sudden comprehension, but there was no stopping his mother.

'Oh, yes,' she exclaimed eagerly. 'I'm sure Miranda's nothing like Sophie.'

'Miranda?' Was he the only one who noticed that Grace's questions were becoming increasingly personal? 'And have you met her?'

'Sadly, no.' Mrs Ferreira gave Oliver a regretful look. 'Not yet, anyway. But I'm sure we'll like her. She's a lawyer, you know? With a very successful career of her own. Unlike Sophie, who has never worked at anything for more than a few weeks that I know of.'

'Nancy!' At last, Oliver's father intervened. 'This is Oliver's business, not ours. I don't think you should be gossiping about things that are really no concern of ours.'

'But they are our concern,' Mrs Ferreira sniffed. 'You want your son to be happy, don't you?'

'Naturally, I do. But by the same token, I don't want to drive him away again because we've been interfering in his life.'

Oliver's mother looked a little anxious now. 'I'm sure he knows I only have his best interests at heart.'

'Yeah.' But Oliver threw his father a grateful glance. 'Let's talk about something else, shall we? I wouldn't want to bore your guest with my problems.'

'I'm not bored,' said Grace at once, but this time she seemed to think better of pursuing it. Her green eyes challenging his, she murmured, 'I suppose I ought to be going. It's getting late and I am finding the change of temperature rather tiring.'

'Oh.' Mrs Ferreira looked disappointed now. But this time she didn't argue. 'Oh, well, if you must.'

'I have enjoyed it,' Grace assured her, getting to her feet, and Oliver and his father did the same. 'The meal was delightful. I'd probably have made do with beans on toast if I was at home.'

His mother looked pleased. 'You must come again,' she said at once. 'Whatever he says, I know Oliver finds our company very dull.'

Somehow he managed to stop himself from saying how he really felt, but he sensed Grace was perfectly aware of his feelings. 'We'll see,' was all she allowed herself. 'But thank you. You're—all—very kind.'

She kissed his father and mother before leaving, but as she started across the patio Mrs Ferreira had the final word. 'Oliver,' she said, looking up at him with wide, ingenuous eyes. 'Why don't you escort Grace back to the villa? It's not far, I know, but it is dark, and she is staying there alone.'

'I—'

He opened his mouth to say he was sure Grace didn't need his escort, when she spoke. 'Oh, that would be kind,' she murmured, her green eyes alight with provocation. 'If you don't mind, that is?'

CHAPTER TEN

How could he refuse?

However much he might want to, he was virtually compelled to accompany her. Just because he didn't want to be alone with her, just because he had spent the whole evening convincing himself that whatever unholy attraction he felt towards her, he could conquer it, was no reason to be rude.

And refusing to escort her would be rude. And awkward. And arouse the kind of questions he didn't want to answer. Already his mother and father were looking at him expectantly, waiting for him to say the obvious: that he'd be delighted to accompany her, that he was sorry he hadn't thought of it himself.

The trouble was, he suspected Grace had only agreed to it because she'd known how he would feel. Well, some of it anyway. She probably thought he would resent her audacity, or maybe that it would annoy him. Annoy him? God! He wished he could sustain his anger towards her. It would be so much easier, so much healthier.

'No problem,' he said at last, choosing the least fulsome form of acceptance. 'Shall we go?'

If Grace was surprised at his easy compliance, she didn't show it. 'Thanks, again,' she said, raising a hand in farewell, and preceded him along the path that led around the side of the villa.

They crossed the lawn at the front of the house and then circled the Lovells' garden to where a crushed shell path led up to the front entrance. A pillared portico shaded double doors, and Grace pulled a key out of her purse, ready to let herself inside.

112

'Well—thanks for coming with me,' she said coolly, giving him a swift appraising glance. 'I guess I can manage from here.'

'Sure?' He wasn't inclined to let her have it all her own way. 'Wouldn't you like me to check inside, in case there's a prowler lurking on the premises?'

'That won't be necessary,' began Grace confidently and then caught her breath on a sudden gasp. 'Oh, God!'

'What?' Oliver was instantly alert. 'What's wrong? Are you feeling ill or something?'

'No.' Grace swallowed and pointed through the glass panel that edged the door. 'There's a light on inside.'

So there was. Oliver's eyebrows drew together. 'And you didn't leave a light on, right?' he asked softly.

'No.' She shook her head.

'So—' Oliver hesitated '—is there an alarm?'

'There is, but I didn't activate it,' she confessed in a low voice.

Good thinking, thought Oliver sardonically. But still, she had only been visiting next door.

'Okay,' he said after a moment, and taking her key out of her hand, he inserted it silently into the lock. 'You stay here.'

'What?' Grace licked her lips. 'No, I can't do that. I can't let you go in there all alone. It—it might be a burglar. He could be armed.'

'And you'll do what if he is?' whispered Oliver drily. 'Pull out your gun and shoot him?'

'I don't have a—oh, you!' She nudged his back instinctively, and then seemed to remember this was no game. 'Um—you will take care, won't you?'

'I didn't know you cared,' he murmured, turning the key and pressing the door inward. But despite his humour, he couldn't help wishing he did have something to use as a weapon if he needed it. Quashing that thought, he positioned her on one side of the door, out of sight of any intruder. 'Just stay here, right. Don't move.'

'But—'

'Do it,' he commanded harshly and, stepping over the threshold, he entered the house.

The light was coming from the back of the house. If he had to guess, he'd say it emanated from the kitchen, and he wondered what a thief could possibly hope to find there. Still, he'd heard of people hiding valuables in the freezer, and it was always possible that an intruder was rifling the fridge, too.

Fortunately his feet made little sound on the marble tiles of the hall. He edged along the wall, one step at a time, trying to get his head around the layout of the house as he did so. It was dark, but the moonlight illuminated a spacious living room through an archway off the hall. A curving staircase was of some concern, but he couldn't worry about that now. If there was anyone upstairs, he would have to deal with it later. Right now, he was intent on his first objective.

He had almost reached the kitchen door when he realised that it was ajar. That was how they'd been able to see the light from outside. But he also realised that they'd been wrong. The light wasn't coming from the kitchen at all. It was shining through the windows from outside. Someone, or something—a cat, maybe—had triggered the security lights and the back of the villa was floodlit by half a dozen halogen beams.

Oliver expelled the breath he'd hardly been aware he was holding. The intruder—if there had been an intruder, and he rather doubted it—was long gone. There had been no attempt to enter the house. He shook his head, relieved that he wasn't expected to act the hero, after all.

He was just beginning to breathe easily again when a hand clutched the back of his shirt. Immediately, he was on the alert, his response instantaneous and uncontrolled. He was so hyped by the adrenalin in his blood that he didn't stop to think before reacting. With a muffled oath, he spun round and pinned the person behind him against the wall.

He didn't know which of them was the most shocked. The whimper Grace gave as his arm pressed against her neck was piteous and he gave a frustrated groan as he realised exactly who he was abusing.

'God, Grace,' he muttered, his arm moving from her throat to support his weight against the wall beside her. His elbow snagged on a switch and he pressed it down illuminating a swathe of the hall, lit by a bronze-shaded light. 'I'm sorry. I thought you were—'

'An intruder. I know,' Grace supplied as he broke off, her voice a little hoarse from the pressure he'd exerted. 'Silly me!'

'So why the hell didn't you stay where you were?' he demanded, using anger in his own defence. 'I could have broken your neck.'

'I know.' Grace was still slumped against the wall, her cheeks pale in the artificial light. 'But I'd just realised what the light was.' She rubbed her throat with a protective hand. 'I didn't mean to scare you.'

'Scare me?' Oliver couldn't help the wry half laugh that escaped him at her words. 'You really know how to eviscerate a guy, don't you?'

Grace smiled now. 'I didn't mean that the way it sounded,' she demurred. She seemed to become aware of how close they were to one another and levered herself up against the wall. 'I really am grateful.'

How grateful?

The crassness of that thought appalled him, but that didn't stop his eyes from dropping to her mouth. Bare of lipstick now, it was still as luscious as it had looked at the start of the evening, and his fingers moved of their own volition to touch her lips. His thumb invaded her mouth, sensual and possessive, rubbing roughly over the soft flesh he'd exposed.

Her eyes were wide now, watching him as he was watching her, and he couldn't prevent himself from bending towards her and capturing her lower lip between his teeth. He bit down on it, hard, seeing the sudden pain that darkened her gaze. But then, as if she, too, had no control over her actions, she swayed unsteadily towards him.

Her lashes veiled her eyes even as her hands spread against his chest. But if it was an attempt to hold him off, it was a very puny effort. When he moved closer, supporting himself with both hands now, her fingers curled into his shirt almost convulsively.

'Do you want me to go?' he asked, his voice as hoarse as hers had been earlier. But he knew it was a foolish question. There was no way he could let her go again and she knew it.

'Just—just stop talking,' she whispered huskily, and abandoning any attempt to hold his emotions in check, Oliver covered her mouth with his.

Her breasts flattened against his chest, the hands that had been fisted against his stomach sliding up to his shoulders, clutching the hair at his nape.

Her lips parted, allowing his tongue to meet and mate with hers, sharing a mutual dance of provocation. Her nails dug into his neck, revealing how responsive to him she was, and blood surged hotly into his groin. A feeling of reckless hunger swept over him and, bending his arms, he allowed his body to rest against hers.

God, that was good, he thought unsteadily, his erection causing her to part her legs to accommodate him. They fitted together so well, it was as if they'd been made for one another, and he shut his mind to any memory of his brother and the fact that Tom had been here before him.

Holding her face between his hands, he angled his mouth over hers, kissing her again and again, long, drugging kisses that seduced his senses and created a feeling of mindless abandon. He had never been more aroused, hot, engorged, his sex throbbing with an almost painful intensity.

His need was a barely coherent awareness. A desire to be inside her, to feel her slickness, her heat, enveloping him, enclosing him, assuaging the hunger she'd aroused inside him. There'd be no relief until he'd satisfied that hunger. He accepted that now. Accepted it and embraced it.

His hands slid into the silky length of her hair, loving the way the red-gold strands curled about his fingers, soft and sensual. His mouth trailed a searing path from her lips to her ear, his tongue exploring its tender honeycomb, before moving on to her throat. He could feel the pulse beating in her neck, its erratic dance matching his own for rhythm, her shoulder lifting beneath his caress, inviting him to taste her soft flesh.

And he did. Nibbling at her shoulder, he drew an inch of honey-soft skin between his teeth and sucked its sweetness until she gave an involuntary moan. Looking down, his eyes were drawn to the dusky V of the cleavage exposed by the low-cut halter-top and, taking an uneven breath, he allowed his hands to follow his gaze.

He shaped her breasts first, feeling their warmth and fullness even through the sequinned basque. Her nipples were hard when his thumbs brushed over their tips, and he bent his head to bestow a sensual kiss in the hollow between.

But it wasn't enough, not nearly enough. He wanted to strip the bodice away and touch her, not sequinned silk. He wanted to tear his shirt away, too, and feel her breasts against his chest, to rub himself against her until she was as hot and out of control as he was.

There were laces at the back of her neck, he discovered, and when he pulled the ends the halter loosened immediately. But now, she clutched the front of her bodice, as if he had taken a step too far.

'Don't stop me,' he groaned, the idea of having to release her causing an actual ache in the pit of his stomach. He wanted her so badly. It would be agony to let her go.

'No,' she said breathily, but although his heart sank at the word, she reached for his hand. 'This way,' she added, tugging him back along the hall, entering the living room he had glimpsed earlier.

The lights beyond the windows had gone out now and there was only a muted glow from the hall outside to show him where she was taking him. A pair of squashy velvet sofas stood at right angles to a stone fireplace, where unlit candles replaced the hearth. There were Chinese rugs covering the floor, long, undrawn curtains at the windows, and a sound system and hi-fi beside a shelf of CDs.

Grace sank down onto one of the sofas, pulling him down beside her, and now she allowed the sequinned halter-top to fall to her waist. Her expression wasn't easy to read in the shadowy light that spilled over them, but he thought she looked a little shocked at her own behaviour. He had the ridiculous notion that she'd never done anything like this before, but then desire and his own need overrode any doubts he might be entertaining.

Her breasts were firm and tips tilted, the nipples as rich and rosy-dark as he remembered. Swollen with her emotions, they jutted proudly towards him, and with another groan he covered them with his hands.

'You are so—beautiful,' he whispered in a shaken voice, suddenly as nervous as she seemed to be. He traced the curve of her throat with an unsteady finger and stared at her with searching eyes. He wanted so much from this woman, he realised uneasily, but he had no idea what she wanted of him.

Yet when her hand lifted and she cradled his jawline, every nerve in his body responded. Her cool hand inflamed him, set him on fire, and he turned his face into her palm. He kissed her there, and then along her arm to her elbow, his tongue finding the sensitive veins within. She quivered beneath his caress before saying huskily, 'Take off your shirt. I want to see you.' And buttons flew as he wrenched the garment out of his trousers.

She drew back, but only as far as the cushions behind her, and Oliver went after her, delighting in the feel of her hard nipples against his chest. They brushed against the triangle of hair that arrowed down to his navel, and he was desperate to feel every inch of her naked body yielding beneath him on their impromptu bed.

His mouth found hers again. He felt as if he was unable to get enough of her, and her tongue was a willing participant in her surrender. He leant over her, stretching his length beside her, allowing his hand to run caressingly from her shoulder to her knee. The split skirt made it easy for him to stroke the inner curve of her thigh and her legs splayed almost involuntarily, just inviting him to lodge one of his between them.

He did so willingly, his thigh moving up to rub against her softness, and he heard the muffled cry she stifled against his shoulder as he did so. Her legs came together again, trapping him in that most intimate of places, and he experienced a similar kind of anguish at her honesty.

Dipping his head, he sought one distended breast, tugging the nipple into his mouth. He suckled greedily, loving the sensation of her tender flesh responding to his tongue, and then moved to her other breast and repeated the caress.

She arched towards him, her bare arms tight about his neck, and Oliver groaned deep in his throat. She was so receptive, so sensitive to his needs, and he wouldn't have been human if he hadn't felt a sense of urgency as his hands moved to her waist.

They trembled slightly as he released the button on her skirt and he was momentarily diverted by the ruby ring that pierced her naval. But then he touched the low waistband of her briefs, and when his hand slid inside the scrap of silk the awareness of how aroused she was drove all other thoughts from his head. Her instinctive reaction was to press herself against his hand, and his fingers slipped naturally between the curls that protected her mound to find the moist cleft they were hiding.

'Oh, God, Oliver,' she choked when he allowed two fingers to invade the cleft, and when his thumb found the swollen nub of her womanhood and rubbed against it she bucked uncontrollably beneath his hands.

'You—you shouldn't,' she breathed when she was able to speak again. But Oliver only buried his face in her softness, delighting in the taste of her passion.

'Why not?' he breathed at last, easing her skirt and briefs down over her hips, and she lifted herself again to make it easier for him. 'You enjoyed it, didn't you?' He pointedly raised his thumb to his lips. 'You seemed to, anyway.'

'But you're still dressed,' she protested, her face flushed and adorable in the half-light. Her hands reached towards his belt. 'Let me help you.'

Oliver expelled a strangled breath when she touched the thrusting mound of his erection. Pausing in her efforts to unbuckle his belt, she let her fingers shape its form and substance, before moving on to his zip.

'Show me,' she whispered, her lips soft and parted in anticipation and Oliver had never known such a sense of excitement as he felt now. He barely managed to loosen the button at his waist before her hands slipped into his shorts. Soft fingers closed around him, moved up and down his length, discovered the pearl of moisture at its tip and brought it her lips.

'Don't,' he said unsteadily, forced to stop her. Getting up from the sofa, he pushed both his trousers and his shorts down his legs, kicked off his shoes. 'Just let me…'

He was down beside her again before he finished his sentence. Covering her with his body, he let her feel the different textures of hair and skin as they touched and mingled with hers. He nudged her legs apart, one thigh nestling against her mound, and she trembled beneath him.

For a few moments it was enough just to lie there and enjoy the unfamiliar intimacy of her body against his. Her breath was warm on his jawline, her breathing catching just a little as she anticipated what was to come. Her hands dipped into the hollow of his spine before exploring the tight muscles of his buttocks. Her nails dug into him, arousing sensations he'd never felt before, and his erection became an almost painful reality.

It was the way she moved beneath him that did it. The feel of her foot sliding the length of his calf, the sensuous shifting of her body. The heady scent of her arousal made his senses spin, and his shaft tightened instinctively. He'd wanted her before, but nothing like this. Now he knew he had to have her or die in the attempt.

Straddling her hips, he lifted himself above her and saw the way her eyes were drawn to his swollen shaft. But when she looked up into his taut face, there was no apprehension in her gaze, no regret. Just a fervent excitement to match his own.

He looked down at her possessively, covering her breasts with his hands again, loving the feeling of power it gave him. She was his, he thought exultantly. Whatever had gone before, she was his now.

'Do it,' she whispered tremulously, lifting her knees, exposing herself completely, and desire overwhelmed any possibility of delaying the moment.

Kneeling between her legs, he guided himself to her slick threshold, nudging the damp curls aside and pressing gently into her.

She was tight, so tight, he might almost have believed she was a virgin. But there was no hidden barrier to his invasion, only muscles that flexed and expanded to accommodate him, only her breathless little cries urging him on.

It was hard to be patient, hard to slow his need to be inside her. Yet it was incredible, too, a previously unknown delight in prolonging her pleasure and his own.

But eventually, he was totally encased in her hot sheath. Despite a momentary fear that he might hurt her, her body had welcomed his entry, and briefly he was reluctant to move.

As if she understood his feelings, Grace reached up to brush his lips with hers. He felt his stubble scratch her chin in passing, but she didn't seem to mind. Her tongue darted to meet his with gentle urgency, and he was consumed by the desire to make this as good for her as it was for him.

Bracing himself, with a hand at either side of her head, he withdrew almost to the point of detachment and felt her instinctive surge towards him. Then, looking down, he pushed into her again and, almost helplessly it seemed, she arched upwards to meet his thrust.

They were perfectly matched, he thought, repeating the action and feeling her muscles tighten around him. For every movement he made, she had an equal response, and pretty soon the desire to prolong their pleasure was swamped by the hunger of his own needs.

Even so, he was determined that she should stay with him every step of the way. Quickening his strokes, he slipped a hand between them and massaged the throbbing nubbin he had caressed before.

Her response was immediate. Clutching his shoulders she gave a breathless cry. As her climax drenched him with her essence, his own control snapped. Slamming into her one last time, he exploded in a paroxysm of feeling, his release spilling out of him and into her with no thought of holding back.

He collapsed on top of her, his body shuddering with the aftershocks of his orgasm, and it wasn't until she shifted a little protestingly beneath his weight that he realised what he'd done. He'd made love to her without giving any thought to protection, hers or his own, and he felt an immediate sense of remorse. She deserved better of him and he ought to be ashamed.

Yet he also knew that to have stopped at any point would have been beyond him. He'd been wrapped in the mindless web of passion and desire and he'd wanted to feel her around him, flesh to flesh and skin to skin. And if that meant there'd be consequences, then so be it. Right at this moment, he thought no price too great to pay.

But when he turned his head and nuzzled her neck, Grace reacted differently. Instead of welcoming his caress, she struggled to throw him off her, and when he obediently rolled onto his side she scrambled off the sofa with a distinct lack of reluctance.

Bending to gather up her clothes, she clutched them to her as she looked down at him, and he was astounded to see that her eyes were red, as if she'd been crying.

'I think you'd better go,' she said tightly, and Oliver was instantly aware of his own nakedness—and of the fact that his sex was still throbbing in a semi-aroused state.

'If that's what you want,' he said, not really understanding the look she was giving him. Sitting up, he reached for his trousers, pulling them on, shoving his shorts into his pocket. He stood up. 'Are you—that is, are you okay?'

'Why wouldn't I be?' she asked in the same strained

voice. She waited until he'd pulled his shirt over his shoulders and then glanced about her. 'Have you got everything?'

'Grace—'

'Just go,' she insisted, gesturing towards the door. 'Your mother and father will be wondering where you are.'

'To hell with my mother and father,' he said harshly, confusion bringing a note of resentment to his voice, and she shook her head.

'Yes. You would say that,' she murmured bitterly. 'Good night, Oliver. Drop the latch on the door as you go out.'

CHAPTER ELEVEN

GRACE slept surprisingly well. After what had occurred, she'd expected to lie awake half the night, but it didn't happen. Exhaustion gripped her, and after washing her face and cleaning her teeth, she tumbled gratefully into bed and into a dreamless oblivion.

Because she hadn't drawn her bedroom curtains the night before, the morning sunlight awakened her. Flooding into the room, it invaded her flickering lids, alerting her to the fact that it was morning.

It was still early, of course, barely seven o'clock, but Grace didn't linger between the sheets. She felt hot and sticky with the aftermath of Oliver's lovemaking, and she was appalled at herself for not showering before she went to bed.

Now, she stepped eagerly beneath the cooling spray, soaping every inch of her body to remove every trace of Oliver's touch. She removed the navel ring she had worn, too, feeling as if she would like to drop it into the waste bin. Whatever, she felt sure she would never wear it again.

Despite her efforts, she seemed to have the taste of Oliver in her mouth, his scent in her lungs. She felt as if she inhaled his distinctive male aroma every time she took a breath, and deciding she needed some fresh air, she decided to go for a jog along the beach.

But before she did so she stripped her bed of its sheets and dumped them in the washing machine. Leaving coffee perking on the hob, she went upstairs again and dressed in a hot pink vest and black bikers' shorts, plaiting her hair while it was still damp.

She only paused long enough to drink a cup of the freshly made coffee before collecting her father's car keys from the drawer in the den, and going through the connecting door into the double garage. She'd decided not to walk down to the village in case she ran into Oliver. If she took her father's car, she could choose her own destination.

There didn't seem to be anyone about next door, she saw as she drove away from the villa. Perhaps the Ferreiras were having a lie-in after entertaining the night before. Despite herself, she couldn't deny the sudden frisson of awareness she felt at the thought of Oliver lying in bed. She didn't think she'd ever forget how she'd last seen him, stretched out on her parents' sofa. Talk about naked and unashamed, she thought tensely. She'd never known a man who was more comfortable in his skin.

But then, she hadn't seen a lot of men naked, she acknowledged. Until last night, she'd never even known what all the fuss was about. Girls she'd worked with had talked about sex—sometimes to distraction—but Grace had always believed their stories were over-exaggerated. An excuse for extolling the exciting lives they purported to lead.

Now she wasn't so willing to dismiss their claims out of hand. However much she might regret what had happened—and she did regret it, bitterly—she couldn't deny that for the first time in her life she felt like a real woman.

Oliver had done that for her. Whatever else he'd done—and she couldn't forget that only the day before he'd told her he wasn't free, that there was some other woman in his life—he'd given her a master-class in the art of seduction.

From the moment he'd touched her in the hall of the villa, until she'd belatedly come to her senses pinned beneath him on the sofa, she'd been lost to all reason, lost to all decency. She hadn't been able to control what had happened any more, she suspected, than he had. They'd behaved shamelessly, caring for nothing but their own selfish gratification. Her lips twisted. And she'd been worried that Tom might make a move on her. Compared to his brother, Tom was an amateur.

Not that that excused her behaviour. As she drove through the outskirts of the village she admitted she'd been as guilty of betraying someone else as he had. She'd known he couldn't be trusted, yet she'd let him get under her skin. She'd already sampled his brand of loyalty, but that hadn't stopped her from giving in.

Which was all the more galling considering she'd spent the early part of the evening thinking of ways she could get her own back for the way he'd treated her the previous morning. She'd dressed up for the occasion deliberately, wanting him to see what he was missing. She'd wanted to humiliate him. That was why she'd agreed to let him escort her home. She'd planned on coming on to him and then spurning any advances he might make.

But then she'd seen what she'd thought was an intruder in her house and all thought of playing the siren had gone out of the window. Not that that would have been a particularly successful option, she acknowledged now. She had the uncomfortable feeling that, however she'd got into Oliver's arms, the end result would have been the same. The man had the ability to blank her mind of all rational thinking. Her only recourse seemed to be to keep her distance from him, which was why she was seriously thinking of returning to England today.

There were few people around and, although Grace had intended to venture farther afield, the empty expanse of the beach persuaded her not to be such a coward. She doubted if Oliver would be up and about this early in the morning. If he was, she would just have to bite the bullet and deal with it.

After all, was she really going to let him drive her back to England? She mustn't forget she had Tom to deal with when she got back. He wasn't going to be pleased when he discovered she was looking for alternative accommodation, and there was still the problem of Sophie's demands putting the future of the garden centre in jeopardy.

She frowned. Perhaps she ought to go to her parents' house instead of back to Northumberland. Her mother and father would be pleased to see her and she could always make some excuse about feeling homesick.

Parking her car beside the sea wall, she sat for a few minutes just staring at the tide rippling along the shoreline. It would be so easy to blame Oliver for all of it, she brooded. If he hadn't married Sophie, if he hadn't neglected her so that she'd turned to Tom for comfort, none of this might have happened.

But was that just wishful thinking? She only had Tom's word that Oliver had neglected his wife and, judging by Sophie's eagerness to retake her marriage vows, it was unlikely to be the whole story. People had to take responsibility for their own actions. Everyone made mistakes. As she'd done, she admitted freely, pushing open her door and getting out of the car.

Kicking off her shoes, she dropped them on the floor of the vehicle before locking the door. Then, swinging one leg over the sea wall, she jumped down onto the sand.

Despite her determination not to think of him, she couldn't help wondering what Oliver's girlfriend was like as she paddled in the shallows. Miranda. Her nose wrinkled in disdain. Why did all the most successful women have such girly names? Mrs Ferreira had said Miranda was a lawyer. Lawyers should be called Sylvia or Elizabeth, solid, sensible names that inspired confidence in their clients. Not Miranda, that sounded as if its owner might be a fey, delicate creature, dependent on a man for protection.

Grace scuffed a toe into the damp sand. Of course, for all she knew Miranda might be exactly that type of woman.

Just because she had a law degree didn't mean she couldn't be both delicate and feminine. Oliver evidently approved of her. Despite his apparent weakness where Grace was concerned, he'd never denied he was committed to someone else.

A lawyer! Grace scowled. That was probably the right profession for his girlfriend to have. Miranda could be relied upon to keep him out of trouble, she thought maliciously. A lover and an advocate, all in one package.

Which reminded her that taking a lover could be a dangerous indulgence. Okay, the chance of her getting pregnant at this particular time of the month was fairly unlikely, but the doubt was there. No doubt Oliver expected she was on the pill. Why wouldn't he? He had such a low opinion of her sexual proclivities anyway, he was prepared to believe anything of her. She shouldn't forget he still believed she was Tom's mistress.

She knew she shouldn't care what Oliver thought, but she did. She didn't like the feeling that she'd been used, however willing she'd been at the time. She'd take damn good care that she wasn't 'used' again.

It was after nine when she got back to the villa. And despite all her soul-searching, she still hadn't decided what she was going to do. Part of her believed it would be cowardly to leave and let Oliver think he had scared her away, but the other part—the greater part, if she was honest—needed to put some space between them for her own peace of mind.

She parked the car on the forecourt and was just fishing her shoes off the floor when she became aware of someone crossing the lawn between her parents' villa and the villa next door. She didn't need to turn to know it was Oliver. Her skin was prickling with awareness and her palms were suddenly damp with sweat.

Dammit, she thought resentfully. Couldn't he at least

have had the decency to let her get into the house without tormenting her again?

Ignoring him, she gathered her shoes in one hand and locked the car with the other. It was just a handful of steps to the door. Could she possibly get inside and shut the door before he realised what she was doing?

No.

Deciding there was no way she could avoid acknowledging him at least, she cast a cool glance over her shoulder as she walked towards the porch. 'Did you want something?'

There was some satisfaction in seeing the way his expression mirrored his surprise at her greeting. But then he gathered himself and said evenly, 'We need to talk.'

'Do we?'

Somehow Grace managed to sound as if she didn't know what he was talking about, and Oliver frowned. 'You know we do.'

'Why?' Grace reached the door and started feeling in the pocket of her shorts for the key. 'I won't tell your girlfriend about last night, if that's what you're worried about.'

Oliver swore then, and Grace realised smugly that she'd snagged a nerve. 'That's not what I meant.'

'No?' Feeling as if she was in control now, Grace arched a mocking brow. 'She must be very sure of herself if she doesn't care that you sleep around behind her back.'

'I don't sleep around,' snapped Oliver grimly. 'And you're not going to provoke me into saying something I don't mean.' He paused, breathing heavily. 'I meant, we need to talk about what happened.'

'Well, not now, eh?' Grace pretended a nonchalance she was far from feeling. 'I need a shower and breakfast, not necessarily in that order.' She inserted the key in the lock, hoping he didn't notice the slight tremor in her fingers as she did so. 'See you—'

He moved towards her so quickly, she didn't have time to pull her key out of the lock again and step inside before his loafer-clad foot was wedged in the doorway. 'You can't avoid me for ever,' he told her flatly as she backed away along the hall. 'We are going to talk, Grace. Now, or at some other time. It's your call.'

Grace's newfound confidence evaporated. 'I've told you,' she said tensely. 'We've got nothing to talk about.'

'I disagree.' He took his foot out of the doorway now that there was no resistance from her. 'I want to know what happened last night.'

Grace caught her breath. 'Oh,' she said, half hysterically. 'Why didn't you say so? Well, I can tell you that.' She paused for a breath. 'We had sex. Good sex, as it happens. I'm sorry. Did I forget to thank you?'

She didn't understand the word Oliver used then, but she suspected it was a Spanish expletive. Whatever, it served the dual purpose of expunging his frustration and gratifying her.

Then, with a baffled gesture, he turned away, allowing the door to slam in his wake.

Although Grace would have much preferred to pack up and go home after that unfortunate little confrontation, she refused to let Oliver's attitude intimidate her. She didn't have to see him again, she told herself. If she got any further invitations from his parents, she'd find some excuse and refuse. In any case, she doubted Oliver would allow them to interfere in his life again.

All the same, she took extra care when she was leaving or returning to the villa. She didn't want to offend the older Ferreiras, particularly as her own parents were on such good terms with them. In consequence, for the next couple of days she lived an almost hermit-like existence, spending only a small portion of the day beside the pool, and then only when she was fairly sure Oliver wasn't about.

She saw him, of course. Unlike her, he seemed to feel no obligation to stay out of her way. She lost count of the number of times she glimpsed him, tall and dark and disturbing, either lounging about the patio next door or strolling casually past the villa on his way down to the village. She thought he took an unholy delight in exposing his lean, muscular torso to her covert gaze, and in her more malevolent moments she suspected he knew she watched him and was enjoying the notoriety.

Then one morning, about a week after Oliver's arrival, she supposed, Grace pulled herself out of the pool to the sound of voices from next door's patio. A man and a woman were talking and she didn't need to see the dark head bent towards his companion to know it was Oliver. The other voice wasn't his mother's, however, and it only took Grace a moment to realise he was speaking to Sophie, his ex-wife.

Despite herself, Grace's stomach hollowed. What was Sophie doing here? Had the Ferreiras invited her? That didn't seem likely after what Mrs Ferreira had said. Oliver, then? Surely not. What about Miranda? Or didn't he care about anyone but himself?

She couldn't hear what they were saying. Nor would she want to, she assured herself grimly, wrapping the towel she'd left beside the pool around her. They were welcome to one another. All she wanted to do was get into the villa without being seen.

Which proved surprisingly easy. Her neighbours were too engrossed in their conversation to pay any attention to her and she slipped through the French doors without attracting anyone's attention.

But as she showered in her bathroom Grace was aware of an unfamiliar twinge of an emotion she didn't want to recognise. She wasn't jealous, she told herself fiercely. She couldn't be. What she and Oliver had shared had been sex, nothing more. Emotion hadn't entered into it. And she was going to get herself into serious trouble if she allowed herself to think of him in those terms.

She was making herself a salad for lunch when someone tapped on the kitchen window. She'd been engrossed in what she was doing, her thoughts miles away, and the sudden summons startled her. But what startled her more was the fact that it was Oliver, particularly after the uncomfortably heated thoughts she'd been having about him.

She couldn't ignore him, however. When he gestured for her to open the door, she obediently dried her hands and went to do as he asked.

'Yes?'

The word was hardly welcoming and his expression briefly registered his dislike of her curt greeting. Then, with an obvious effort to ignore it, he said, 'May I come in?'

Grace moistened her lips. 'Why?'

'I want to talk to you.' Her involuntary withdrawal aroused a momentary fire in his eyes, but he controlled it. 'No. Not about that,' he said flatly. 'I think I got the message there.' He paused. 'This is something else.'

'What?'

'If you'll let me in, I'll tell you.'

'If this is some ploy—'

'It's not.'

Grace pressed her lips together. The trouble was, he had such an honest face. It made her want to believe him. And, truthfully, she was greedy for the sight of him. But that was dangerous and she knew it. Which was why her tone was offhand as she stepped aside and said carelessly, 'Okay.'

But the kitchen, spacious though it was, seemed too small with him in it, and, besides, these surroundings had connotations she didn't want to remember right now.

The living room was similarly out of bounds. So she let him into her father's den, a comfortable masculine room with a couple of leather armchairs, a book-lined cabinet and a mahogany desk, presently clear of anything except the computer that her father couldn't live without.

Even so, Oliver's presence made her instantly aware of the intimacy. His skin seemed darker, probably due to the time he was spending outdoors, his legs long and muscular below the narrow cuffs of his khaki shorts. His shirt had sleeves for once, something for which she was grateful, but as it was open halfway down his chest, he still looked incredibly male and sexy.

'Wh—what do you want?' she asked, putting the width of the desk between them, and Oliver's mouth compressed at her obviously defensive retreat.

'Can I sit down?'

'Why not?'

Grace wished he would, actually. Maybe then she wouldn't feel so intimidated by his presence. But she'd remain standing.

Oliver swung one of the leather chairs round and dropped into it. Then, hooking one ankle across his knee, he looked about him with evident interest. 'This is nice. Your father's sanctuary, I presume?'

Grace took a deep breath. 'You didn't come here to discuss the appointments of the villa, Oliver. What do you want?'

Oliver considered her thoroughly before replying. Then, after bringing an unwelcome flush of colour to her throat, he said, 'Are you all right? You look—tired. Aren't you sleeping well?'

'You wish!' The words were out before she could prevent them and she gritted her teeth in annoyance. Then, swallowing her outrage, she squared her shoulders. 'Get to the point, Oliver. Your wife will be wondering where you are.'

'I don't have a wife.' Oliver gave her a weary look. 'But I guessed you'd seen her. And don't look at me like that. I didn't invite her.'

'Do you think I care?'

But her voice gave her away and she knew he'd noticed when he said drily, 'I thought you might. You and she having so much in common.'

Grace gasped. 'I have nothing in common with that— that—' She broke off, trying to temper her outburst. 'She's nothing like me!'

'You think not?' Oliver was still regarding her with a jaundiced eye. 'Oh, well, if you say so. And I'm sure Tom would agree with you. Where he's concerned, Sophie appears to have sprouted horns and a forked tail! Was that before or after you came on the scene, I wonder?'

Grace stiffened. 'I have no intention of discussing Tom's affairs with you.'

'*Affairs* being the operative word,' remarked Oliver drily, and Grace wanted to punch him. 'Anyway, enough of Tom's emotional hang-ups—did you know that he intended approaching a money-lender for the money to pay Sophie?'

Grace blinked, momentarily taken aback by the sudden change of topic. 'I—why, no. Why would I?'

Oliver allowed his foot to drop to the floor and leaned towards her, his forearms resting along his spread thighs. 'Well, now,' he said coolly, 'I would have thought he'd have taken you into his confidence. You deal with the garden centre's finances, don't you? You seem to know all about it.'

'You flatter me,' said Grace tightly. 'How Tom finances the centre is his business, not mine.'

'Right.' Oliver regarded her intently. 'So you knew nothing about this proposed loan?'

'No.' Grace hesitated. 'No more than you, anyway. You knew he'd been to see his bank manager.'

'George Green?'

'Oh, yes, I forgot.' Grace's lips curled. 'He's a friend of yours, isn't he? Didn't he tell you how desperate for money your brother was?'

'George doesn't divulge his clients' financial affairs,' retorted Oliver grimly. 'Are you saying he turned him down?'

'Why don't you ask Tom?' demanded Grace, feeling resentful. 'Or Sophie? I imagine that's where all this has come from.'

Oliver didn't immediately answer her, but she could tell from the scowl that darkened his features that she was right.

Then, with evident reluctance, he said, 'She told me, yes.' He paused. 'She says she's worried he's going to get himself into real trouble if he goes ahead with it.'

'Good old Sophie,' muttered Grace, guessing this had been her excuse for coming here. 'She's all heart!'

Oliver had been staring at a spot on the floor, midway between his feet, but now he looked up, his eyes wary. 'You don't believe her?'

'I didn't say that.' Grace sighed. Then, giving in to the desire to tell him the truth, 'All right, it may be true. Your friend Mr Green was only willing to advance Tom half of what he needed. Go figure.'

'Only half?'

'Yes.' Grace considered a moment before adding, 'Tom has taken on quite a lot of debt in recent months, what with the expansion and everything. I'd say any bank would fight shy of increasing his liability.'

'Yeah.' Oliver absorbed this. 'So you think Sophie was right to come and tell me?'

Grace shook her head. 'I don't know what Sophie's motives are.'

'But you don't like her much, do you?'

Grace sighed. 'I don't have to like her. She's your problem, not mine.'

Oliver's sigh was regretful. 'What if I said she was Tom's problem? What then?'

'I'd say that was wishful thinking,' replied Grace, wishing she'd never got into this. She came round the desk, hoping he would get the message and get to his feet. 'Well, if that's all…'

'It's not.' Using the wheels on the chair to propel himself forward, Oliver slid across the hardwood floor towards her, capturing both her hands before she could get away. 'When can I see you again?'

Grace's breath caught in her throat. 'I—you're seeing me now,' she protested, but Oliver only pulled her between his thighs, trapping her there, with his hands moving familiarly to cup the rounded curve of her bottom.

'You know what I mean,' he said, his voice muffled as he pressed his face against her bare midriff. 'I want to be with you. Since we were—together, I haven't been able to think of anything else.'

Nor had she!

'Not—not even Miranda?' she asked in a strangled voice, not really knowing why she cared. She ought to put a stop to this right now. Only she seemed incapable of doing so.

Oliver uttered a savage oath. 'Forget Miranda,' he muttered, lifting his head and nuzzling the damp hollow between her breasts. 'I have.'

For now, Grace thought, aware of the ambivalence of his words. He was making no promises, no commitment. She didn't doubt he wanted her. She could feel the hard length of him throbbing against her leg. But for how long? she wondered bitterly. It was not something she wanted to find out.

'Well, I haven't,' she declared resolutely. 'And unless

you want to risk possible impotency—' her knee brushed deliberately against his erection '—I think you'd better go.'

But the threat was a hollow one, and he seemed to know it. Instead of letting her go, his fingers slid beneath the cuff of her shorts, cool against her hot flesh. Then, as he lifted one hand to her nape with the obvious intention of pulling her face down to his, chimes echoed throughout the house.

'Someone's at the door,' said Grace unsteadily, not sure whether she was glad or sorry, and Oliver was forced to let her move away to answer it.

'Saved by the bell,' he said harshly as she stumbled towards the door. 'But we're not finished, Grace. And that's a promise.'

CHAPTER TWELVE

GRACE flew back to London the following day. She desperately needed to get her feelings about Oliver into perspective and she didn't trust herself to keep him at arm's length when he was only next door. She didn't trust him either, but that was another story.

As far as she knew, Sophie was still staying with the Ferreiras, and that was another reason for getting away. She had been downright rude when she'd come looking for Oliver the day before, leaving Grace in no doubt that she blamed her for delaying him.

If she only knew, Grace mused a little bitterly as she waited for her luggage to appear on the carousel. Goodness knew what might have happened if Sophie hadn't interrupted them. Which was why she'd wasted no time before packing her cases and ringing the airport.

After collecting her bags, Grace waited another twenty minutes for a taxi and then gave the driver her parents' address in Croydon. She'd decided to spend a couple of days with them before returning to Northumberland. And if that meant she was a scaredy-cat, then so be it. She needed to get her head together, and she wasn't going to do that if Tom decided he'd waited long enough to make his intentions known.

Of course, it meant delaying finding a place of her own, but that couldn't be helped. She just wished Tom could get his financial problems solved so that she wasn't made to feel she was deserting a sinking ship.

And she wasn't deserting him, she assured herself. And nor was the ship sinking, whatever Sophie said. She was simply moving out of Tom's house. So no one should be under any illusions as to why she'd been staying there.

Only her mother was at home when she reached the house in Maple Terrace. The narrow Victorian townhouse looked exactly the same as always, and she was relieved to know that some things never changed.

Her mother wasn't expecting her and she looked very surprised when her daughter hauled her suitcases into the hall. 'I thought you were supposed to be in Spain, darling,' she said, viewing Grace's pale face with some misgivings. 'Is something wrong?'

'No.' Grace knew she sounded defensive, but she couldn't help it. 'I just thought I'd spend a few days with my family before going back to work. That's all right, isn't it?'

'Of course.' Mrs Lovell's response was reassuringly swift. 'I just can't imagine anyone preferring grey old London to sunny San Luis.' She paused. 'Was Tom with you?'

'Tom!' Grace's ejaculation was terse. 'No! No, Tom wasn't with me. Why would you think he was?'

'Oh…' Mrs Lovell looked a little discomfited. 'I just thought he might be. I—er—I was speaking to Nancy on the phone a couple of days ago and she said her son was staying with them at the moment. I naturally assumed she meant Tom.'

'Well, she didn't,' said Grace, dumping her backpack on top of the cases. 'Look, can I have a cup of tea? I didn't have anything on the plane.'

'Sorry, darling.' Her mother pulled a wry face. 'Here am I prattling on about the Ferreiras, and you're dying of thirst. Come along. Come into the kitchen. I'll make you some lunch.'

'A cup of tea will do,' said Grace, following her along the hall. 'Then I'll get unpacked.'

'As you wish.'

Mrs Lovell led the way into a pleasant kitchen-cum-breakfast room that looked out onto the pretty walled garden at the back of the house. Gesturing Grace towards a chair, she went to fill the kettle, and after it was plugged in she gave her daughter a bright smile.

'So,' she said, 'did you enjoy your holiday?'

Grace expelled a slow breath. 'I—very much,' she said. 'Um—how's Dad?'

'He's okay.' But it was obvious Mrs Lovell wasn't interested in discussing her own affairs. 'So—what did you do?'

'Not a lot.' Grace sighed, and then, realising that wasn't going to satisfy her mother, she added, 'I swam and sunbathed. Did a little walking. It was too hot to do much else.'

'And did you see the Ferreiras?'

'I had supper with them one evening.'

'And how are they?'

Grace felt like saying 'Don't you know?' as her mother had recently spoken to Mrs Ferreira, but she didn't want to create any animosity between them.

'They're fine,' she said instead. 'Looking good.'

Mrs Lovell nodded. 'So it was Oliver who was staying with them?'

'Yes,' said Grace tightly, remembering why she had moved out of her parents' house in the first place. Her mother always insisted on knowing the far end of everything.

'So how was he?' Mrs Lovell paused. 'I don't suppose Sophie was with him?'

'They're divorced, Mum,' exclaimed Grace shortly, realising as she said that it was important for her to believe it, too. 'Oh, good. The kettle's boiling.'

Mrs Lovell went to make the tea, but when she turned back again, Grace could tell from her expression that she wasn't deceived by her daughter's rather inept attempt to change the subject. 'There is something wrong, isn't there?' she said, taking a jug of milk out of the fridge and setting it on the pine table. 'I suppose it's Tom. I knew it as soon as Nancy told me that Sophie had moved out of the house.'

'What? What did you know?' Grace felt helpless in the face of her mother's certainty. 'I'm not involved with Tom, if that's what you're implying. I've never been involved with him and I have no intention of getting involved with him. Is that clear enough for you?'

'There's no need to take that tone with me, Grace.' Her mother was looking offended now. 'Just because Tom doesn't return your feelings—'

'Tom's a jerk!' Grace interrupted her hotly. 'Sometimes I don't even like him very much.'

'You say that now,' declared Mrs Lovell placidly, pushing the cup of tea she'd just poured towards her daughter. 'But I know you, darling. You wouldn't have gone dashing off to Spain like that, with no warning, if you hadn't been upset about something.'

Grace stared at her disbelievingly. 'You really think I'm interested in Tom?'

'Well, you have to admit, you got along with him very well last summer. After all, if you hadn't, he wouldn't have offered you a job and—'

'The job has nothing to do with it,' exclaimed Grace incredulously. Then, deciding she was going to get no peace until she came clean about Tom's intentions, she heaved a sigh. 'All right. If you must know Tom is the reason I went out to Spain.'

'I thought so.' Her mother looked smug.

'But it's not how you think,' Grace insisted grimly. 'Since Sophie left, things have been—difficult. I don't like living in the house alone with him. I don't trust him. He seems to think it's only a matter of time before we become—well, an item, if you know what I mean. And that's not going to happen.'

Mrs Lovell frowned now. 'He hasn't threatened you, has he?'

'Of course not.' Grace gave a weary shake of her head. 'But he is intent on giving people the impression that I'm his girlfriend. And I'm not. That's why I've decided to get a place of my own.'

'You're leaving the garden centre?'

'Not the job, no. Not unless he fires me, that is.' She grimaced, considering the thought. 'I suppose he might. If he thought he could get away with it.'

'Oh, dear me!' Her mother shook her head. 'I had no idea Tom was like that.'

'Didn't you?' Grace's tone was dry. 'You haven't forgotten Sophie was married to Oliver when Tom started seeing her, have you?'

'Well, no.' The older woman chewed on her lower lip. 'But he's always maintained that she and Oliver were having problems before he got involved.'

Grace shrugged, wishing she could believe that. 'Perhaps they were,' she said, sipping her tea. 'Anyway, it's no concern of ours, is it?'

'I suppose not.' Mrs Lovell took a deep breath. 'So—what are you going to do? Find somewhere else to stay before you return to work?'

Grace wished she could, but that didn't seem likely. 'I—probably not,' she said at last. 'I'll think about it.' She paused. 'But for now, can I stay here? For a couple of days, I mean?'

'As if you need to ask,' declared her mother reprovingly. 'You're always welcome here. You know that. Your father will be delighted to have his little girl back again.'

'Not so little,' murmured Grace drily, finishing her tea. 'Thanks, Mum. I knew I could count on you.'

*   *   *

Oliver discovered Grace had gone that evening. He hadn't seen her about but he'd assumed she was keeping out of his way. It wasn't until he'd driven Sophie to the airport late in the afternoon that he'd called at the villa next door and discovered the place was locked and empty.

Frustration ate at him as he realised that Grace had gone without even telling him what she planned to do. She'd returned to England—and Tom—leaving him feeling like a fool.

All the same, he made an immediate decision to follow her example. Even though he'd given Sophie a message to deliver to his brother in the hope of buying the time to prolong his holiday, that was no longer an option. With Grace gone, he was unsettled and angry, and one way or another he determined to settle this once and for all.

His parents were sorry he wasn't staying on. 'There's no reason for you to get back,' George Ferreira protested. 'So long as Sophie gets her money, she'll be happy, and Tom ought to consider himself very lucky that he's got a brother who's prepared to forgive and forget and save his miserable neck! I know I am. Staying on here means everything to me, son. I won't forget this.'

Oliver shook his head. 'I've done little enough for you in the past, Dad,' he said firmly. 'And you've done a lot for me. I'm only happy to have a chance to repay you.'

'Even so…'

'Look, I think I'd better get back,' said Oliver gently. 'I've been away long enough. Andy's going to think I've taken early retirement.'

'And there's Miranda to think of,' put in his mother slyly. 'I expect she's missed you.'

'Yeah.'

Oliver managed a faint self-deprecatory smile, but in all honesty Miranda's needs were not high on his list of priorities. He would have to see her. He owed it to her to explain in person why their affair was over. Whatever happened with Grace—and he wasn't entirely convinced that he was doing the right thing in pursuing a woman who might still be his brother's mistress—his association with Miranda couldn't go on.

He blew out a rueful breath. He had the suspicion he was kidding himself by implying that he had any choice where Grace was concerned. When he was with her, there was no denying the hold she had on his emotions. No matter what happened, she'd proved to him that what he'd had with both Sophie and Miranda was just a pale shadow of how things could be. But whether that was enough, for either of them, he had yet to find out.

One thing was sure, he had no intention of sharing her with his brother. If she was still involved with Tom, then that would be his cue to back off. It would be painful. There was no doubt about that. But he'd survive it, he assured himself. He'd survived other disasters in his life and he was older and wiser now than he'd been four years ago.

Another alternative occurred to him during the flight back to England. He could sever any connection with Grace and save himself any more soul-searching. Which sounded all very well in theory, but would be harder to achieve in practice. He'd have to think about that.

It was late afternoon when he arrived back at his apartment. He'd phoned Mrs Jackson before he left San Luis to warn her of his return and she'd kindly stocked the fridge for him. He was able to make himself a sandwich before phoning Andy, and then after assuring his partner that he'd be back in the office the next morning, he went to unpack.

The phone rang as he was considering what to do about dinner. There was steak in the fridge, but he wasn't in the mood for cooking it himself. Conversely, he had little enthusiasm about going out for a meal. He could always phone for a take-away, of course, but he couldn't decide what he wanted to eat.

He answered the phone with some reluctance. He doubted Grace would be phoning him—he hadn't given her his number—and there was no one else he wanted to speak to tonight. But on the off chance that it might be his mother, phoning to assure herself that he was home safely, he picked up the handset.

'Ferreira.'

'So you're back!'

It was Tom and Oliver's stomach hollowed. What now? But, 'Yeah,' he answered civilly. 'Have you been trying to reach me?'

'Only for the last week.' Tom was aggressive. 'I gather you've been on holiday.'

'Is that a crime?' Oliver refused to let him rile him. 'I've been staying with Mum and Dad, actually. But, of course, you'll know that.'

'Yeah, I know.' But Tom didn't sound any the less aggrieved. 'Sophie gave me your message.'

'Good.' Oliver nodded to himself before adding evenly, 'I'll have George sort out all the details, but basically all I'm doing is securing your loan. You don't owe me anything.'

'Don't I?' There was still that militant note in his brother's voice. 'Do you think because you've got me out of some deep crap that I don't have any feelings?'

Oliver blew out a breath. 'Look, Tom, I don't expect any gratitude. But, yeah, I did think you might be pleased.'

'What about?' Tom snorted. 'The fact that you've been seeing Grace behind my back?'

'Ah.' Oliver was beginning to understand his brother's attitude now and he didn't like it one little bit. 'Did she tell you that?'

'Yeah.' Tom paused as if considering the alternative. 'Isn't it true?'

But Oliver had no intention of discussing anything Grace had said with him. The very fact that she'd told Tom about them seeing one another proved that she was still very much involved with the other man, and right now what he really wanted to do was ram the phone down his brother's throat.

'Why don't you ask her?' he demanded harshly, and before Tom could say anything else he slammed the handset back onto its cradle.

The phone rang again almost immediately, but Oliver didn't answer it. The day had started out badly and had just got worse—much worse—and, abandoning any thought of food, he collected a bottle of single malt from the cabinet and retired to his bedroom.

But the idea of drinking himself into a stupor had no appeal. It wasn't going to solve anything, he realised bitterly as the phone rang yet again. However reluctant he was to see Grace again, he was going to have to bite the bullet and do it. Until then, he'd have no peace, and that was a fact.

CHAPTER THIRTEEN

OLIVER didn't get the chance to visit the garden centre for the next couple of days. His first day back was taken up with catching up on the work that had accumulated in his absence, and although he left for home at six-thirty, it was after midnight before he turned out his light.

Then, the next day Andy sprang a charity awards presentation dinner on him. 'One of us has to go,' he said, dropping the invitation on his partner's desk, 'and Jill and I had to attend the Mastersons' cocktail party last week while you were enjoying yourself in the sun.'

'But it's tonight,' Oliver objected, staring down at the embossed card. 'And I don't have a partner.'

'Then I'd find one pretty damn quick,' retorted Andy unsympathetically. 'What about your tame lawyer? Isn't she available?'

Consequently, and with much reluctance, Oliver phoned Miranda, and later that evening he found himself escorting her into the Gosforth Manor Hotel, where the charity dinner was being held.

'This is nice,' she said, hanging onto his arm as they walked into the convention hall, which had been furnished for the occasion. Dozens of white damask-covered tables shone with silver cutlery and cut glass, the centrepiece on each one a blush-pink-shaded lamp strung with matching roses. 'When do you think we'll be eating? I didn't have time for lunch.'

'Soon, I hope,' said Oliver fervently, using the excuse of having to thread their way between the tables to extricate himself from her clinging fingers. He paused every now

148

and then as various friends and acquaintances attracted his attention, but for once he didn't try to introduce his companion. Then, after finding their table, he seated Miranda beside the wife of a local Conservative councillor before excusing himself and striding back towards the exit.

But even in the foyer of the hotel, he couldn't escape being accosted by people he knew. It was the price of working in a highly publicised industry, and he knew he owed it to Andy to be polite. Nevertheless, all this meeting and greeting didn't go down well in his present mood. He was thinking of abandoning any attempt to grab a few minutes on his own and return to the hall when he saw his brother approaching him with a purposeful expression on his face.

Oliver stifled an oath, but his face must have betrayed how he was feeling because Tom's features briefly assumed a smug look of satisfaction.

'Well, well,' he said, halting beside Oliver and regarding him critically. 'If it isn't my benefactor in person. I assume you expected to meet me here. That's why you haven't returned my calls.'

Oliver felt a momentary twinge of guilt for the calls his answering machine had racked up which he'd ignored. But the fact was, he didn't want to have another row with Tom. They'd only just begun speaking again, for God's sake.

'Look,' he said now, 'this isn't the time or the place to get into this. I'm planning on coming out to Tayford in the next day or two. We can talk then.'

Tom looked as if he was about to argue, but then seemed to think better of it. 'So,' he said, glancing round, 'where's Gracie?'

'Graci— Grace?' Oliver stared at him. 'Why would I know where Grace is?'

'Well, she's with you, isn't she? This is a black-tie affair. We're all expected to bring a partner.'

Oliver bit back the obvious question and said instead, 'No. I haven't seen her.'

Tom scowled. 'What are you telling me, bro? That you and she have broken up already?'

'No. I—' Oliver was at a loss of how to answer him without revealing his feelings, and pride wouldn't let him humble himself before his brother '—I—er—I ought to be getting back.'

'But—'

However, before Tom could dig any deeper, a girl came to take possession of his arm. 'So there you are,' she exclaimed, half reprovingly, pressing her ample breasts against his sleeve. 'I've been looking for you.'

Now it was Tom's turn to look embarrassed and Oliver, waiting for an introduction, realised he knew the girl. It was Gina Robb, the office junior from the garden centre. He fell back a step. Gina! She had to be sixteen at the most. What the hell was Tom thinking about? Was this some ploy to make Grace jealous? Or was he really incapable of being faithful to only one woman, as Sophie had said?

Tom seemed to realise what Oliver was thinking and his fair features filled with hot colour. 'Um—you know Gina, don't you, Oliver?' he muttered as the girl fluttered her mascaraed eyelids at him. Then, to the young woman, 'You remember my brother?'

'Oh, sure.' Gina turned her baby-blue eyes on Oliver now. 'Hello again, Mr Ferreira. We didn't expect to see you here.'

'No.'

Oliver allowed the rueful denial, but Tom was recovering his composure, and he said coolly, 'You didn't tell me who you were with, Oliver? Is it someone I know?'

'It's just a friend,' said Oliver, wishing he'd never had the bright idea of leaving the hall. 'And I'd better be getting back to her.'

'We'll come with you and you can introduce us,' said Tom at once, sensing his brother's reluctance and responding to it. 'You never know, we might be sitting at the same table.'

Grace walked into the office at eight o'clock in the morning, her usual time for starting at the garden centre. She'd spent four days in London with her parents, but now she'd convinced herself that she was ready to get back to work.

It wasn't going to be easy, despite what Tom had said. But the idea of submitting her notice had never really been an option. She wasn't a quitter, and if Tom wanted her to stay on, she was prepared to do so. But, she'd explained, it had to be on her terms, not his.

He hadn't been best pleased when she'd begun by telling him she planned on staying at the bed and breakfast she'd found in Ponteland until she could get a place of her own. He'd objected, of course, but however persuasive he'd been in assuring her that she had nothing to fear from him, she wanted there to be no doubt in anybody's mind—*for anybody, read Oliver*—that there was anything going on between her and his brother. Oliver might be able to share his sexual needs—she refused to call them affections—between two women, but she wasn't like that. Besides, she'd never been attracted to Tom, had never given him or anyone else any reason to believe that she was, and she wanted no more ambivalence about it.

Not that she believed Oliver would care, one way or the other. She had it on good authority that he and Miranda were still seeing one another, and although it tore her up to think of him with another woman, she had to get over it.

That was what she'd told her mother when Mrs Lovell had finally got the truth of what had really happened in Spain out of her. Grace hadn't wanted to tell her parents.

She hadn't wanted to do anything to sour relations between the Lovells and the Ferreiras, but it had been such a relief to confide in someone.

Her mother had been appalled at Oliver's behaviour, until Grace had confessed that she had been as much to blame as he was. She'd actually admitted that she had feelings for Oliver, though she'd also insisted she had no intention of acting on them. He had a girlfriend in England, she'd said, trying to make it sound as if she'd known that all along, and Mrs Lovell had eventually accepted that it had just been an unfortunate lapse of judgment on both their parts.

At least, she'd said she had, Grace had later acknowledged. Her mother knew her too well to be deceived by her daughter's assertion that she'd accepted the situation when she was still so obviously upset. Consequently, she had insisted that Grace phone Tom and explain what she planned to do before travelling back to Northumberland. And even after his reassurances, she'd made Grace promise that should she feel at all uncomfortable with him or Oliver, she would give in her notice.

Grace had chosen not to explain that the chances of her seeing Oliver again were slim, thank goodness. After all, she'd worked at the garden centre for many months without laying eyes on him, and his indifference towards his brother's problems must have renewed the strain on their relationship.

At least she hoped that was so. Dealing with Oliver on a day-to-day basis was not something she wanted to think about. Which was something else she'd kept from her parents.

This morning, however, it was quite a relief to see that the centre was still functioning as efficiently as ever. She hadn't mentioned Tom's financial difficulties to him, deciding that if he wanted to tell her anything he would. But, despite his apparent optimism, she had been half afraid that the company's problems might have leaked into the workplace. She'd dreaded coming back to long faces and the possibility of imminent redundancies.

But apparently that was not to be. When she entered the office, Gina was at her desk, as usual, and Bill Fletcher was helping himself to coffee from the jug that had been simmering on its hotplate.

'Hi.' It was Gina who greeted her, and Grace was surprised. The office junior was usually fairly sullen in the mornings. She could only assume she'd had a good time the night before. 'Tom said you were coming back today.'

Tom? Grace was surprised at the girl's familiarity, but it was up to Tom himself to discipline her if he thought it was necessary.

'Good morning,' she said, including the older man in the salutation. Then, because the coffee at the bed and breakfast had been pretty ghastly that morning, 'Pour me a cup, too, will you, Bill?'

'No problem.' Bill filled another cup and handed it to her. 'Have a good holiday?'

Grace managed a faint smile. 'Not bad,' she said, cradling the cup between her hands. 'Hmm, this is good.'

'You don't look very brown,' remarked Gina critically. 'Wasn't the weather hot?'

'It was very hot, actually,' said Grace firmly. 'Too hot for sunbathing sometimes.'

'Oh, it could never be too hot for me,' exclaimed Gina fervently. 'I love the heat. I can't wait for my holidays.'

Grace moved to her desk, deciding she had more important things to think about than a holiday she desperately didn't want to talk about. She wanted to ask if Tom was in yet. The door to his office wasn't closed, but that could mean anything, and until she'd gauged his attitude and decided whether she was comfortable with it she couldn't be absolutely sure she was staying.

Her question was answered a few moments later when Tom breezed through the door from outside. He had obviously just arrived. He was tossing his car keys in his hand, and when he saw Grace his expression became even more animated.

'Hey,' he said, crossing the office to her desk and standing looking down at her with evident pleasure. 'Welcome back!'

'Thanks.'

Grace permitted herself a glance up at him, and was relieved to see that he looked much as usual. If the financial troubles of the centre were bothering him, he didn't show it, and she envied him his composure. In his position, she thought she'd be tearing out her hair.

'Journey okay?' he asked, referring to the flight she'd taken to Newcastle airport. 'I would have met you, you know. You didn't have to rely on a cab.'

'It was fine,' said Grace, shaking her head, and as she did so she saw Gina regarding them with a puzzled look on her face. She was probably wondering what was going on, reflected Grace. As far as Gina was concerned, Grace was still living in Tom's house. She would have to correct that assumption at the first possible opportunity.

'Well, come into the office,' said Tom, nodding towards his door. 'I've got something I want to tell you.'

Not about Oliver, Grace hoped, getting up from her chair with some reluctance. It was Tom who had told her about seeing Oliver and Miranda together at a charity awards dinner he had attended, and she had no desire to hear any more about them. It was what she'd expected, after all, she told herself, even if the strength of that assertion was wearing very thin.

'You haven't forgotten you're taking me to see the new development at lunchtime, have you, Tom?' Gina asked as he headed towards his office, and Grace saw the irritated glance he cast in the girl's direction.

'I said I'd do it if I had the time,' he declared, stepping back so that Grace could precede him into the office. 'Get me some coffee, will you, babe? I'm parched.'

If looks could have killed, they would both have been struck stone-dead, Grace acknowledged as Tom closed the office door behind them. But he seemed oblivious of—or perhaps indifferent to—Gina's malevolent stare. After ushering Grace to a seat, he dropped into his own chair with apparent complacence.

Then, resting his arms on the desk, he leaned towards her. 'It's good to have you back, Grace. The office hasn't been the same without you.'

'Really?' Grace gave him a dry look. 'You and Gina seem to be on good terms. Since when has she called you "Tom"? It was Mr Ferreira when I went away.'

'Oh, you know Gina.' Tom made a careless gesture. 'She's an airhead. She likes to think that we're close, but you know we're not.'

'It doesn't matter to me one way or the other,' said Grace flatly, and then realised that Gina was standing in the doorway behind her, holding the cup of coffee she'd poured for Tom.

There was an awkward moment when none of them spoke, and then Tom said, 'Oh, is that my coffee, babe? Thanks. You're a good kid.'

Gina's features were set and angry as she passed Grace's chair on her way out, but she didn't look at the other woman. This time, her anger was solely directed towards Tom himself, and Grace hoped she hadn't been responsible for causing a rift between them.

'So,' she said when the door had closed behind the girl, 'what is it you want to tell me?' She almost mentioned the proposed loan, but then realised she wasn't supposed to know about that. She moistened her lips. 'Have you managed to solve your financial problems yet?'

Tom regarded her consideringly. 'Did Oliver tell you?' he asked, and Grace realised she wasn't the only one who had been holding things back. 'You did see him while you were staying in San Luis, didn't you?' He paused. 'And Sophie?'

Grace swallowed, but refusing to be intimidated, she said, 'Did Sophie tell you that?'

'Wasn't she supposed to?'

'I suppose that depends what she told you,' said Grace shortly. Then, realising she was being defensive, she added, 'I don't have to account for my movements to you, Tom. You're my employer, nothing else.'

Tom had the grace to look a little discomfited, but he didn't back down. 'Sophie told me that you and Oliver had been spending time together,' he said. 'Don't you think I have the right to know if you've been screwing my own brother?'

Grace gasped and sprang to her feet. 'If this is the way it's going to be from now on, I think I ought to leave,' she said curtly. 'What I do or don't do is not your concern. But for the record, I haven't been—screwing—anyone!'

What she had shared with Oliver had not been 'screwing', she defended herself. Well, not for her, anyway, and that was what this was all about.

'Okay, okay.' Tom seemed to realise he had gone too far now, and getting to his feet, he gave her an apologetic look. 'Sit down, Grace. I'm sorry if I sound peeved, but you must know how I feel about you. Imagining you with Oliver of all people just cuts me up.'

'I imagine that's much the way he felt when you seduced his wife,' retorted Grace, not giving an inch. 'But I have no intention of making you the guardian of my morals. If— if I want to go out with anyone, I will.'

'Including Oliver.'

'Oliver already has a girlfriend,' she reminded him tersely. 'You told me so yourself.'

'Oh, yeah. Right. Right, he does.' Tom wiped a bead of sweat from his upper lip and appealed to her again. 'Sit down, please. I do want to tell you about the loan. And I promise I won't bring up Oliver's name again.'

Grace hesitated. She suspected deep down this was never going to work. Tom and Oliver had too much history and, whatever happened, she was always going to be a reminder to Tom of what might have been.

But, for now, she subsided into her seat and faced him noncommittally. She did want to know how he intended to rescue the garden centre. Stupidly, she wanted to assure herself that the jobs of all the friends she'd made here would be safe.

'The bank has agreed to extend my loan,' said Tom without any further preamble, resuming his own seat and regarding her expectantly. 'What do you think of that?'

Grace didn't know what to think. Unwillingly, Oliver's reaction when he'd heard of what his brother had proposed came to mind, and she badly wanted to ask if he was instrumental in the bank having a change of heart.

But she couldn't do that without provoking more questions, and if Oliver was involved surely Tom would tell her. For the moment it was enough to know that the future of the garden centre was secure.

'Um—that's great,' she said now, managing to sound as enthusiastic as he expected. 'You must be relieved.'

'Oh, I am.' Tom spoke fervently. 'I knew it was only a matter of time before something turned up.'

Grace reserved judgment on that. She hadn't forgotten how depressed Tom had been when she went away even if he had. But although she waited for him to explain why the bank had agreed to extend its loan, he didn't elaborate, and she decided it was time she got back to work.

Nevertheless, the day seemed endless. Even though she'd thought that getting back into a routine would disperse the gremlins that had been plaguing her ever since she left San Luis, it didn't seem to work that way. She no longer felt at ease here, and blaming it all on Gina—who spent most of the day casting baleful looks in her direction—or Tom, wasn't enough.

She suspected Tom was keeping something from her. He had remained determinedly obtuse about the circumstances surrounding his sudden good fortune, and although he had apparently accepted her decision to find a place of her own, his attitude made her wonder if he actually believed it. He could be so smug at times and she didn't trust him not to have an agenda of his own.

But what agenda? What was he really thinking? She wished she knew.

She was preparing to finish for the day when Gina sidled up to her desk. The girl hadn't spoken to her since their conversation that morning. Grace, who was feeling inordinately weary, hoped she wasn't going to complain to her because Tom hadn't taken her out to see the new development as he'd apparently promised.

Now, waiting for the girl to speak, she knew an almost visceral feeling of apprehension. What now? she wondered anxiously. Whatever it was, she was too tired to care.

'It was the charity awards dinner on Tuesday,' Gina said at last, and Grace arched an inquiring brow. So what? 'Tom invited me to go with him,' the girl continued, this time causing a genuine look of surprise to cross Grace's face. 'Did he tell you?'

'I—no,' Grace said at last, unable to hide her consternation. She'd known Tom had attended the dinner, of course. That was where he'd seen Oliver and Miranda.

Together. But he hadn't mentioned that his date had been his office junior.

'Well, he did,' declared Gina triumphantly. 'And we had a great time!'

'Well—good.' Grace's smile was rueful, but no less warm because of it. It wasn't Gina's fault that Tom was acting like a fool. But it explained a lot. 'I'm glad you enjoyed it.'

'Are you?' Gina regarded her suspiciously now. 'I bet you wish you'd been here. He'd probably have asked you instead of me.'

'Hey, I wouldn't bet on it,' protested Grace quickly, wanting to quash that idea immediately. 'Tom and I are just working colleagues, you know. We don't spend our free time together.'

Gina frowned. 'But you live in his house.'

'Not any more.' Grace paused and then decided the girl deserved an explanation. 'I'm going to get a place of my own. For the present, I'm staying at a bed and breakfast in Ponteland.'

Gina stared at her. 'But—why?'

'Oh…' Grace shook her head. 'I suppose since Sophie moved out, it hasn't been the ideal situation. And I need my own space.'

'So you're not, like—seeing Tom?'

'Socially?' And at Gina's nod. 'No.'

Gina considered this. 'So you're not jealous?'

'No.' Grace was almost amused at that suggestion. Her eyes narrowed. 'Did he say I was?'

'He said a lot of things,' said Gina, looking a little doubtful now. 'He'd been drinking, you see, and I don't think he knew half of what was said.' She sighed. 'Of course, it was mostly about his brother, Oliver.' She paused and then continued cautiously, 'Was that right? Oliver was in Spain when you were there? Tom seemed to think you'd been seeing Oliver behind his back.'

Grace felt a faint flush enter her cheeks. 'I don't think Tom has any business discussing what I did or didn't do when I was on holiday,' she declared tersely. 'As I say, it's nothing to do with him.'

Gina hunched her shoulders. 'He thinks it is.'

'Well, it isn't.' Grace took a deep breath, trying to calm herself. 'In any case, Oliver is seeing someone else. You probably met her. She was with him at this dinner you went to, wasn't she?'

'Oh—Miranda, yeah.' Any spark of hope Grace might have had that Tom had been lying was extinguished by Gina's reply. 'She was there. But I don't think she was very happy.'

'No?' Grace's pulse quickened. 'Why?'

'Oh, she was really mad because Oliver had left her sitting at the table on her own while he went out of the conference hall to talk to someone else. That was where we met him, actually. In the foyer of the hotel. He seemed in no hurry to get back to her.'

'Really?' Grace knew she was clutching at straws, but she couldn't help it. 'Why do you say that?'

Gina hesitated. 'Well, when Tom said he'd like to meet her, Oliver was really reluctant to introduce us.'

'Oh.'

Grace's lips tightened. Now she understood. Naturally Oliver would be reluctant to introduce his girlfriend to his brother. First of all, he'd know that Tom would waste no time in telling her that he'd seen them together, which would prove what a liar Oliver was. And secondly, and probably the more important of the two, he had no reason to trust his brother with a woman he loved.

'Anyway, I'm glad we've had this talk,' Gina said now, and for the first time Grace could remember, she gave the older woman a beaming smile. 'I'll see you tomorrow, right?'

CHAPTER FOURTEEN

OLIVER was sitting at his desk in his riverside apartment, trying somewhat unsuccessfully to make sense of the sheaf of drawings Andy had handed him as he was leaving, when his intercom buzzed.

'Take a look at these and try and drum up some enthusiasm for the project,' Andy had advised him drily. 'And next time you think about taking a holiday, think again. You've been as miserable as sin since you got back.'

It was a fair comment, and as Oliver got up to see who had rung he wondered if his partner had decided he needed more than a five-minute pep talk. Andy was a good friend, and Oliver knew he only had his best interests at heart, but right now he didn't want to see anybody.

Except Grace.

But Grace wasn't available. When he'd driven up to the garden centre the day after the charity dinner, which was a week ago now, he'd discovered that she wasn't there. According to Tom, they'd only been in phone contact since she got back from Spain, and while that was good to hear, the fact that Tom thought she intended dumping this job in favour of other employment in London wasn't. For the present, she was staying with her parents, and that was as much as Tom was prepared to say.

For himself, Oliver had little doubt that he was to blame for Grace's absence. He had behaved abominably, both before and while they were in Spain, and he could hardly blame her if she thought he was all kinds of a heel. He was sure Tom would have lost no time in telling her that he was seeing Miranda again, and he was sure she was never going to believe that it hadn't meant a thing.

Okay, he probably shouldn't have invited Miranda to attend the dinner with him. It hadn't been his most sensible course of action, but Andy had been adamant that he should represent the firm and it had seemed the only solution.

Besides, he'd wanted to speak to Miranda, to explain why they wouldn't be seeing one another again, but obviously a social occasion like a charity dinner hadn't been an intelligent choice of venue. Miranda had got the wrong impression when he'd invited her out, and when he'd finally broken the news to her, she'd taken it badly.

It had been a disastrous evening all round. Tom had been there, enjoying his discomfort, and although Oliver had been relieved that Grace wasn't with him, he had expected Tom to gloat about his discomfort to her when he got home.

Of course, the next day, when he'd shunned one of Andy's policy meetings to drive up to Tayford, he'd discovered that Grace wasn't there either. He suspected Tom had enjoyed that, too, even though Oliver hadn't specifically said he was there to see her. But the fact remained, in spite of his reluctant involvement in the centre's financial affairs, he had had no other excuse for making the trip. And Tom, damn him, knew that.

Now, feeling an intense weariness, he pressed the button on the intercom. 'Yes?'

'Oliver?'

It was a female voice, but not the female voice he wanted to hear and he swore under his breath. 'Sophie,' he said flatly. 'What do you want?'

'Is that any way to greet your wife, Oliver?' Sophie sounded suitably put out. 'Darling, I want to talk to you. May I come up?'

'I can't think of anything we have to say to one another,

Sophie,' said Oliver heavily. 'And you're not my wife either. I'm sorry, but—'

'It's about Grace,' Sophie interrupted him swiftly. 'I'm sure you'll be interested in what I have to say. Press the button, darling. It's starting to rain.'

Oliver hesitated. Despite what she'd said, he couldn't believe that Sophie would know anything more about Grace's intentions than he did. And, right now, he was in no mood to be civil to anyone, least of all his ex-wife.

But still...

Against his better judgment, he pressed the button that released the door in the downstairs warehouse and then crossed the room to send the lift down for her. There was no harm in hearing what she had to tell him, he told himself grimly. After all, Tom was no friend of hers.

Sophie stepped out of the lift exuding her own distinctive brand of perfume, but although she would have reached up to kiss his cheek, Oliver drew back. This was no social call, and Sophie was no friend of his either.

'You're not still working,' she protested, clattering across the hardwood floor on her ridiculously high heels. 'Darling, it's after nine! Even workaholics like you have to relax sometimes.'

Oliver folded his arms across his chest, tucking his fingertips beneath them, regarding her dourly. 'Just say what you have to say, Sophie,' he advised. 'I'm busy.'

'I can see that.' She flicked the papers on his desk with a careless finger. Then she turned to face him. 'Aren't you going to offer me a drink? Or don't you have alcohol on the premises?'

Oliver expelled a heavy sigh. 'This isn't a social call, Sophie,' he said. 'What do you want?'

Sophie pulled a wry face. 'Oh, you are gloomy, aren't you? Tom said you were, but I didn't believe him.'

'Tom?' Oliver scowled. 'Tom sent you here?'

'Oh, heavens no.' Sophie gave a scornful laugh. 'Tom wouldn't do that. He's got far too much to lose.'

Oliver stared at her. 'What are you talking about? I thought you said this was about Grace.'

'It is.' Sophie gave a pitying shake of her head. 'Don't you know your brother is besotted with her? He always has been. Ever since he persuaded her to come and work for him. Why do you think I walked out?'

Oliver felt incredibly tired suddenly. 'I know all this, Sophie. You told me before, remember? You don't need to labour the point.'

'Oh, I think I do.' Sophie glanced around, saw the leather chair that stood in the window embrasure and perched un-invited on the arm. Then, crossing one slim leg over the other, she said, 'I told you Tom was besotted with Grace. I didn't say Grace was besotted with Tom.'

Oliver stiffened. 'That's not what you said before.'

'No, well...' Sophie lifted her shoulders in a careless gesture. 'We all have our weaknesses. But Tom did let you think she was his mistress, didn't he?' She bent her head. 'Perhaps I believed it, too.'

Oliver uttered an oath. 'Are you saying it wasn't true?'

Sophie shrugged. 'Maybe,' she said cautiously, noticing his darkening expression and responding to it.

'Are you or aren't you?'

Oliver was in no mood to suffer her prevarications and Sophie made a defensive little gesture. 'All right,' she admitted in a small voice. 'For what it's worth, I think I was wrong.'

Oliver took an angry step towards her and then controlled himself. 'So why the hell didn't you say anything? Why did you walk out, for God's sake?'

'Oh, well, if you think I'd want to stay with a man who couldn't take his eyes off another woman, you're very much mistaken,' exclaimed Sophie, looking a little indignant now. 'He made a fool of me, Oliver, and no man does something like that and gets away with it.'

Oliver made a choked sound. 'Is that why you insisted that you wanted to take your money out of the centre?' he exclaimed, beginning to understand. 'Because you knew that was the one way you could get back at him!'

Sophie neither admitted nor denied it, and Oliver stared at her with incredulity in his eyes. 'But why?' he said, shaking his head. 'Why are you telling me this? You've got your money, or you're getting it, at any rate. Why tell me this now?'

'Because you bailed him out,' said Sophie shortly. 'I wanted him to suffer, but you made it easy for him.' She grimaced. 'It was the only thing I could do.'

Oliver was stunned. 'My God, you meant what you said, didn't you, Sophie? No one makes a fool of you without reaping the punishment.'

'What goes around comes around,' said Sophie carelessly. 'Besides, maybe I'm feeling generous. I heard you'd finished with Ms Sawyer and I wondered if the reason you hadn't seen Grace since you got back from Spain was because you were reluctant to do something your brother didn't think twice about.'

'And that was?'

'Seducing your wife?' suggested Sophie drily. 'Whatever he may have told you, Oliver, I was not to blame for what happened. All right, I may not have put up much resistance. I was tired of being a corporate widow, of you working every hour God sent—as you still appear to do, by the way. But make no mistake, your brother has no scruples, none whatsoever, and it's about time someone gave him a taste of his own medicine.'

'That would be me, right?' Oliver shook his head. 'Well, don't hold your breath. Grace isn't coming back to the garden centre. According to Tom, she's going to stay in London.'

'And you believed that?' Sophie was aghast. 'Oh, Oliver, didn't you know? Tom never gives up. He still wants Grace. You know he does. And he's prepared to do just about anything to get her. Including—and particularly—keeping you two apart.'

It was after midnight by the time Oliver got to the bed and breakfast in Ponteland. But he wasn't tired any more. He was invigorated. Not least because he'd hauled his brother's ass out of bed and threatened to beat him to within an inch of his life if he didn't give him Grace's address pronto.

Tom had tried to bluff it out, of course. He'd attempted to convince his brother that Grace had said she wasn't coming back, and that when she'd turned up a few days ago, he'd been as surprised as anyone.

But it was all lies, and Oliver knew it. Sophie had told him that Grace had returned to the garden centre the day after his visit, and eventually Tom had had to give in.

All the same, Oliver couldn't help feeling a twinge of apprehension as he stood outside the neat little terrace house where Grace was staying. He knew he'd acted impulsively in coming here tonight, and the resolution that had carried him this far was suddenly losing its impetus.

What if she refused to see him? What if she didn't believe him when he told her how he felt about her? She had no reason to trust him. He'd let her down before. And with Tom spreading his lies about him, she was bound to think the worst.

God! Oliver raked back his hair with an unsteady hand. He should have waited until the morning to come here. Things always looked better in daylight. Turning up on someone's doorstep in the dead of night was just asking for trouble. What if her landlady called the police? What if she had him arrested? What explanation was he going to give for being here? That he was a lovesick imbecile? Yeah, Andy would love that!

But something, some compulsion that was stronger than his inhibitions, had him laying a hand on the gate, lifting the latch, pushing it open. The path was short, just a couple of flagstones with a square of lawn on one side and a privet hedge on the other. He reached the door, saw there was no bell, and rapped the knocker.

The sound was absurdly loud in the stillness of the lamplit street and he glanced about him, convinced he must have awakened half the neighbourhood. But nothing stirred, not even the cat blinking at him from its place on next-door's step. There wasn't a soul about, not outside or inside apparently. He would have to knock again and risk disturbing all the occupants of the house, or give up.

The latter seemed the more sensible option. He stepped back to give the place one final once-over and suddenly saw a movement at an upstairs window. A curtain had been drawn aside and someone was peering down at him. A woman.

Grace!

It was her, and as he stared up at her he felt a rekindling of the exhilaration he had felt earlier. Gesturing frantically, he tried to convey the fact that he wanted her to come down and speak to him, but before she had a chance to respond the door in front of him opened. A woman of perhaps fifty confronted him, henna-coloured hair confined in a hairnet, a towelling dressing gown wrapped tightly about her well-endowed figure.

'Do you know what time it is?' she demanded, as if finding a strange man on her doorstep at one o'clock in the morning was her only objection. 'What do you want?' She looked towards the gate and saw the Porsche parked at the

kerb, and her expression changed. 'I've got no vacancies.
I'm sorry.'

'I haven't come to ask for a room,' said Oliver, with a
smile, realising he mustn't alienate the woman. 'Actually,
a friend of mine is staying here and I wondered if I could
have a word with her.'

A frown pulled the woman's plucked brows together. 'A
friend of yours?' she echoed. 'A woman friend?'

'That's right.'

'I'm sorry, I don't allow callers of the opposite sex in
rooms after ten o'clock.'

As if time mattered, thought Oliver impatiently. If one
of her boarders wanted to commit an offence they could
do so equally well before ten as after.

'Then perhaps you have a sitting room, or a lounge,
somewhere where we could talk.'

'At this time of night?' The woman gave him a pained
look. 'I don't think so.'

'Please…' Oliver was trying desperately to control the
urge he had to push past the woman and charge up the
stairs to Grace's room. 'It's very important.'

'As I say—'

'It's all right, Mrs Lawson, I'll speak to him at the door.'
To Oliver's relief, Grace appeared behind the woman, but
her expression was not encouraging. 'What do you want,
Oliver? Is it the garden centre? Has there been some trouble?'

'No.' Oliver spoke harshly, but he couldn't help it. If she
thought they were going to conduct a conversation with her
landlady looking on, she was very much mistaken. 'Grace,
I need to talk to you.'

Grace regarded him with hostile eyes. 'Then I'm sure it
can wait till morning,' she said crisply. 'I'll be at work at
eight o'clock—'

'To hell with work!' Oliver realised he was hardly helping his cause by losing his temper, but he couldn't seem to help it. 'Grace, I want to speak to you. I have to speak to you. Goddammit, I didn't even know you were back until a couple of hours ago.'

'And that matters why?'

Oliver made a strangled sound. 'Are you kidding me?' He cast a fulminating look at Mrs Lawson. 'Grace, don't do this to me. Do you think I'd have come here at this time of night if it wasn't urgent?'

'I don't know what you might do,' she replied coldly. 'I still don't know why you've come at all.' Her lips tightened. 'Unless this is the only time you can speak to me without your girlfriend finding out.'

'Dammit, I don't have a girlfriend,' snapped Oliver angrily. 'And if Tom told you I have, he's wrong.' He gave Mrs Lawson another killing glance and then added grimly, 'As a matter of fact, I haven't slept with Miranda since I realised how I felt about you.'

He saw Grace's cheeks deepen with becoming colour. And although he resented having to speak of his feelings in front of the landlady, he felt a glimmer of hope stir inside him at this evidence of her response.

'Tom let me think you weren't coming back,' he added, pushing his advantage. 'He wants to keep us apart.'

'I—I don't know…' She sounded doubtful. Then, 'How did you find out I was back?'

Oliver sighed, knowing this wasn't going to please her. 'Sophie told me,' he said flatly. 'She came to see me tonight.'

'Sophie?' As he'd expected, Grace became wary. 'Why would Sophie tell you something like that?'

But Oliver had had enough of his uninvited audience. 'Come with me and I'll tell you,' he said, looking challengingly at the landlady. 'If your watchdog will let you.'

'Now look here—' began Mrs Lawson indignantly, but Grace interrupted her.

'I'll get dressed,' she said, surprising them both. 'Don't worry, Mrs Lawson. I'll be okay.' Her eyes moved to Oliver again. 'Will you wait?'

Oliver's lips twisted. 'For ever, if necessary,' he said drily. 'I'll be in the car.'

Five minutes later, Grace opened the passenger door and slid in beside him. She had shed the quilted dressing gown she'd been wearing earlier in favour of jeans and a chunky purple sweater. And although she'd attempted to comb the front of her hair, her braid looked just as wispy as it had done when she'd joined them at the door.

'Okay,' she said a little breathlessly. 'Tell me about Sophie. Why did she come to see you?'

Oliver took a deep breath. 'Not here, hmm? Will you come back to my apartment?'

'Your apartment?' Grace swallowed. 'Can't we talk here?'

'Did you expect we would?'

Grace gave him a reluctant look. 'I guess not.'

'So?'

She regarded him for another long moment and he wondered if she could see his heart in his eyes. Then she said softly, 'Okay. But will you bring me back here afterwards?'

'If you want to come,' said Oliver, not trusting himself to touch her, even though he badly wanted to. He flicked the ignition. 'Thanks.'

Grace frowned as he pulled away. 'What are you thanking me for?'

'For believing me,' he said simply. 'You do believe me, don't you? About Miranda, I mean.'

Grace was silent for a long minute. Then, as they pulled out onto the main road south she said, 'You have seen her since you got back from Spain.' It was a statement, not a question, and Oliver sighed.

'You mean the charity dinner?' And at her silent acknowledgement, 'That was a mistake. I realised it as soon as I picked her up.'

'Then why did you invite her?'

'Oh—' Oliver shook his head '—I knew I had to talk to her. I knew I had to tell her that we couldn't go on seeing one another, and when Andy dropped the dinner invitation in my lap, so to speak, that seemed as good a time as any.'

'But it wasn't?'

'No.' Oliver's tone was flat. 'I thought I could handle it delicately, but I couldn't. Being with her felt wrong, and I was trying to get away from her when I ran into Tom and Gina in the foyer.' He paused. 'Tom told you he'd seen us, didn't he?' He made a bitter sound. 'That was manna from heaven for him.'

Grace frowned. 'Never mind Tom. Tell me about Miranda. What did she say?'

Oliver sighed again. 'Well, she was hurt, naturally. She realised I'd just used her.' He grimaced. 'I wasn't very proud of myself, I can tell you.'

'Do you regret it?'

'Regret what?' He gave her a startled look.

'Breaking up with Miranda.'

'Hell, no.' Oliver was fervent. 'I've known for weeks that it wasn't working any more.'

'Because of me?'

Grace said the words tentatively, and Oliver took his eyes from the road to stare at her shadowy profile. 'Do you doubt it?' he demanded. 'Dammit, Grace, don't you know how I feel about you by now?'

He was forced to look back at the road then, and he sensed rather than saw the way her hands clenched together in her lap. 'In—in Spain, you said you weren't free,' she said huskily.

'I wasn't.'

'I know. But you didn't say anything about finishing with her.'

'No.' Oliver was honest. 'I didn't do that.'

'Why?'

'Because I was a fool.' Oliver groaned. 'Look, I thought you and Tom—well, you know what I thought. That day I came to the house and you were there.' He shook his head. 'What else was I supposed to think? Tom practically naked and you flushed as if you'd just come out of the shower.' He lifted his shoulders in a weary gesture. 'I wanted to kill you both.'

Grace bent her head. 'Tom wanted you to think that.'

'I know. I've got the picture now. Yet, even then, I couldn't keep away from you. But by the time we got to-gether in Spain, I was afraid I was getting in too deep. I still believed you and Tom were together, and I was deter-mined not to let him make a fool of me again.'

Grace was silent for a moment. Then she said quietly, 'Why didn't you ask me?'

Oliver's fingers tightened on the wheel. 'I suppose I was afraid to.' He stared at the road ahead. 'I'll be honest. After the divorce, I swore I'd never trust another woman again. I didn't want to get involved with you. I knew from the start that you could hurt me far more than Sophie ever could. So I used Miranda. As a barrier. I let you think I cared about her. But I never did. Not in this way.'

Grace wet her lips. 'What way?'

Oliver gave her a disbelieving look. 'You know,' he said roughly. 'As soon as you'd left San Luis, I knew I'd made the biggest mistake of my life. Believe it or not, I didn't care whether you and Tom had ever been together any more. I wanted you, I needed you. Goddammit, I loved you—*love* you. Everything else is just so much hot air.'

'Oliver—'

'Don't say anything, please,' he begged her desperately, hearing what he was very much afraid was regret in her voice. 'Can we wait until we get there to continue this? I don't think I can take any more disappointments, not behind the wheel of a car, anyway. I promised myself I wouldn't say anything until we got there. Hearing you, seeing you, and not being able to touch you is driving me insane.'

He heard the uneven catch in her breathing, sensed that she was as eager to reach their destination as he was. But all she said was, 'Just tell me why Sophie came to see you. I didn't know you and she were on visiting terms.'

'We're not.' Oliver's voice was harsh. He sighed again. 'All right, she has a grudge against Tom, and she thought I was staying away from you out of some crazy notion of loyalty.'

'But you weren't.'

'Hell, no.' Oliver was vehement about that. 'I came to see you at the garden centre the day after the charity dinner, but you were not there. That was when Tom told me you'd decided not to come back—'

'What?'

'That you were going to find another job in London.'

Grace gasped. 'But that's not true.'

'No. That was what Sophie told me.' He hesitated. 'She also told me she'd been jealous of you, and that that was why she'd demanded her money back.'

'But she's got her money back now.'

'Yeah, but she thinks it was too easy for him. She knew I'd guaranteed his loan, and—'

'*You* guaranteed the loan?'

Oliver glanced sideways at her. 'Didn't he tell you?'

'No.' Grace shook her head.

For a moment, Oliver didn't know what to say. 'I was sure he would.'

'You shouldn't be sure of anything where Tom is concerned,' said Grace quietly, and Oliver nodded.

'Ain't that the truth?' he muttered. 'Dammit, why do we have to have traffic lights every hundred yards at this time of night?'

'They're not every hundred yards,' Grace protested, and he was reassured to hear a trace of humour in her voice. 'Is it much farther?'

'Not far,' he promised, taking the road down to the quayside. 'We're almost there.'

He parked the car outside the warehouse. At any other time, he'd have stowed it in the adjoining garage, but right now even his beloved Porsche couldn't take precedence over his need to be with Grace. Unlocking the warehouse, he led her across the concrete floor to the lift and then pushed the button for the first floor.

There was a light in the lift, but it was dull and muted, and he didn't intend to touch her until he could see what was in her eyes.

'Cool,' she said, when she stepped out of the lift into his loft apartment. She moved to the windows, looking out at the lights of the city across the water. 'What a view!'

'It's better in daylight,' said Oliver, securing the lock and shedding the leather jacket he'd been wearing. He dropped it onto a teak chest and then walked across the floor to turn on a pair of lamps. He was feeling as nervous as a schoolboy. 'Can I get you anything to drink?'

Grace turned from the windows. 'At nearly two o'clock in the morning?' she said wryly. 'I don't think so.'

'Okay.' Oliver lifted one hand to ease the tension at the back of his neck. 'So—I guess you want to talk.'

'That is why you've brought me here,' she reminded him

softly, but Oliver thought he detected the humour in her voice again. She hesitated a moment and then came slowly back to where he was standing. 'Unless you've got a better idea.'

Oliver's throat felt dry. 'I can only think of one better idea,' he said hoarsely, and felt his blood thicken when she lifted a hand to stroke the roughening curve of his jawline.

'So can I,' she said, reaching up to trace his lips with her tongue. 'We can talk later.' She paused and then added breathily, 'Let's go to bed.'

CHAPTER FIFTEEN

IT WAS light outside the long windows when Grace opened her eyes. It was going to be a brilliant early summer day, she thought sleepily, and although it was barely six o'clock the sun was already pushing its way into the room.

It illuminated the room, with its high vaulted ceiling, illuminated the huge bed, where she was lying, illuminated the still-prone form of the man who was lying beside her, whose lean, muscled thigh imprisoned hers beneath him.

For a moment, Grace knew a sense of panic, her brain immediately jumping to the horrifying conclusion that Tom had forced his way into her bed during the night. But then, the memory of the previous night's events swept over her in blissful detail, and the knowledge that it was Oliver who was beside her, Oliver who had made bewitching love to her all night, sent a shiver of delighted anticipation through her body.

She tried to turn her head to look at him, but his head was resting on the curtain of her hair spread out across his pillow and it wasn't easy. His breathing, slow and easy, was a delightful counterpoint to the quickening beat of her heart as she inched towards him, and her lips curved in a smile of utter satisfaction. She loved him, she thought incredulously. She could let herself admit it now. She loved him with every fibre of her being and she felt so grateful to Sophie for wanting to get her own back on Tom. Without her intervention, it might have been weeks, months, before she and Oliver saw one another again, with all the possible doubts and misunderstandings between.

Doubts and misunderstandings that Tom would have seized upon to achieve his own ends.

'What are you thinking about?'

Oliver's husky query startled her. She'd assumed he was still asleep, but evidently he wasn't, and she drew a tremulous little breath as she turned more fully towards him.

'What do you think I was thinking about?' she countered, her eyes soft and sensuous as they rested on his lean dark face. 'You, of course. I was thinking about last night, about you bringing me here.'

Oliver rolled onto his side facing her. 'Do you regret it?'

Grace caught her breath then. 'No.' She swallowed anxiously. 'Do you?'

'Only that I didn't do it sooner,' said Oliver, his hand cupping her nape to bring her nearer. 'So why were you looking so troubled? I saw the way your smile faded, as if you'd remembered something you didn't like.'

Grace's lips tilted. 'You weren't supposed to have been watching me,' she reproved him. 'I thought you were asleep.'

'What? When I've just spent the most incredible night of my life, and the woman I spent it with is lying beside me?' Oliver chided her gently, bringing a trace of colour to her cheeks. 'I still can't believe you're here with me. I've wanted you for—well, it seems like for ever.'

Grace put out her hand to touch his cheek, but he captured it in one of his and brought her palm to his lips. 'I love you,' he said, his voice thick with emotion now. 'I never want to let you go.'

'You won't have to,' she murmured, nestling closer. 'I love you, too. Isn't that just perfect?'

'Perfect, yes.'

But Oliver was looking at her as he spoke, his hand seeking her hip, pulling her against him, letting her feel the effect she had on him. His breathing wasn't slow and easy now, it had quickened like hers, and his mouth on hers was hot and demanding.

The impact of his kiss was as devastating as ever. Its heat spread over her, flooding her with a need to match his own. Her legs parted at the first nudge of his knee and she rode his thigh shamelessly, feeling her arousal wet against his leg.

And although she was still tender from their lovemaking of the night before, she was as eager as he was to repeat the experience. She wanted him, wanted to know that wonderful sublimation of self she'd felt when he was inside her, the feeling that they were not two, but one.

He was gentle with her, easing his way into her tight honeycomb with indefinite patience. But she welcomed his penetration, her muscles at first expanding and then contracting around him so that his breath caught in his throat.

'God, oh, God,' he muttered as she arched towards him, unable to prevent the automatic response of his body. Grace lifted her slim legs and wrapped them about his waist and he had to steel himself not to lose control. But when he felt her climax rippling about him, drenching him in her essence, his release was a spontaneous reaction. He spilled himself into her with a groan of complete and sensual satisfaction.

It was a long while after that before he moved again, and Grace stretched luxuriously when he eventually rolled onto his back beside her. She had never felt happier, more content, and although she was loath to break this up, it was after nine o'clock and they couldn't stay in bed all day.

'Where are you going?' Oliver protested when she threw the covers aside and made to get out of bed, and she cast him a lazy glance.

'For a shower,' she said, nodding towards the open door of the bathroom across the room. 'I assume you do have a shower, don't you?'

'Oh, yeah, I have a shower,' he agreed ruefully. His eyes caressed her. 'Perhaps I'll join you. But I'm going to make some coffee first. I need something to get me going.' An attractive smile crossed his lips. 'You've worn me out.'

Grace's lips parted in mock indignation. 'I've worn you out?' she exclaimed, flinging herself across the bed and straddling him threateningly. 'You're insatiable!'

'Are you complaining?' he asked, his hands sliding up the sides of her body from her hips to her breasts. 'I rather got the impression that you liked it.'

'I did. I do. Oh…' Grace was too susceptible to his caresses to do anything but collapse upon him, and once again Oliver rolled over, pinning her beneath him. 'You know I do.'

'Mmm.' Oliver contented himself with nibbling at the soft slope of her breast. 'I know. I like it, too. Too much, probably.' His lips twisted. 'I don't want to let you go.'

Grace gazed up at him with her heart in her eyes. 'You don't have to let me go,' she told him huskily. 'I'm here as long as you want me.'

'Do you mean that?' He smoothed the tumble of her hair back from her cheek. 'You know, I dreamed of this. Of seeing your hair spread across my pillow, of making love with you. And now you're here and I can't quite believe how lucky I am.'

Grace trembled. 'Oh, Oliver…'

'Yeah. Pathetic, isn't it? It must be nearly twenty years since I had dreams like that.'

'I think it's wonderful,' she told him sincerely. 'I'd given up believing I could feel like this about anyone. And now…'

'And now?'

She wound her arms about his neck. 'And now I can't imagine my life without you,' she confessed shyly. 'That's what I was thinking before, when you thought I looked troubled. If it hadn't been for Sophie wanting her revenge, we might never have known how we felt.'

Oliver stroked her lips with his thumb. 'It's possible,' he admitted honestly. 'I must admit, when Tom told me you weren't coming back to the garden centre, I was shattered. I was sure I was responsible for you deciding to move away and, short of asking Tom for your address, which I was too proud to do, I didn't know how to get in touch with you. Until tonight, of course. Sophie didn't have your address either, and I rousted Tom out of his bed to get it.'

Grace shook her head. 'I was sure you'd just been using me, that Miranda was really the woman you loved.'

Oliver bent his head and kissed her then, his lips lingering against hers. 'Tom has a lot to answer for,' he said roughly. 'But I can afford to be generous. After all, you hadn't left the garden centre and sooner or later I'd have found out you were still there.'

Grace managed a tremulous smile. 'I suppose so.'

'I know so,' said Oliver firmly. 'Don't forget, we had unfinished business.'

'And is it finished now?' she asked, propping herself up on her elbows as he pushed himself up and swung his legs over the side of the bed.

'It'll never be finished,' he assured her, leaning over the bed and swinging her up into his arms. 'Come on, I'll help you with your shower.' He carried her into the bathroom and set her on her feet. 'Then we'll go and see Andy. He's my partner in the business. I know he'll be glad to hear the good news. He thinks I've been as miserable as sin since I got back from Spain.'

Grace dimpled. 'And Tom?'

'Yeah. Tom, too,' agreed Oliver drily. 'I want to see his face when I tell him where you're going to be living from now on.'

*   *   *

Almost exactly a year later, Oliver and Grace were returning from having dinner with Oliver's parents at their villa in San Luis. In a few days, Grace's parents were coming out to join them, but for the present they had the place to themselves.

And just like on that other occasion when Oliver had escorted her home, Grace saw lights burning in the house where they shouldn't have been.

'Juanita never uses the living room,' she protested, when Oliver suggested the maid might have lit them. 'In any case, it doesn't look like a lamp. Oh, God, Oliver, you don't think someone's broken into the house!'

'No.' Oliver was reassuringly calm. He inserted his key in the lock and opened the door. 'Stop panicking. There's a perfectly reasonable explanation.'

'What explanation?' exclaimed Grace, unconvinced, urging him on so that she could get past him and reach the stairs. 'I'm going to—'

'Wait.' Oliver captured her arm as she would have rushed away, and drew her along the hall to the living room. 'Let's see what it is first.'

Grace cast him a nervous look. 'But Alex—'

'Alex is all right. You know he is. Maria would have rung us if—'

But before he had time to finish what he was saying, Grace had uttered an incredulous gasp. Halting in the arched entrance to the living room, she gazed in wonder at the sight that confronted her. Dozens of candles had been placed around the room, their flickering flames the source of the illumination she had glimpsed from outside. As well as the candles, long-stemmed roses decorated every available surface, their beauty only surpassed by their fragrance.

Grace's lips parted and she turned to look at her husband with wide, uncomprehending eyes. 'Who—who—?' And seeing his complacent expression, 'Did you do this?'

'Well, I'd be feeling pretty annoyed if I hadn't,' he remarked drily. 'Do you like it?'

Grace shook her head in amazement, turning back to look at the room again. 'But how could you?' she protested. 'We've been at your parents' villa all evening.'

'Except for when I came back to check on Alex,' Oliver reminded her smugly. 'Our son is safe in his cot, by the way. And Maria's reading in the dressing room, just as you expected.'

Grace turned to him then, a look of adoration on her face. 'And you did this for me?'

'For both of us,' he said, taking her shoulders and bending his head to bestow a tender kiss at the corner of her mouth. 'Don't you know what day it is?'

Grace frowned. 'Well, it's not our wedding anniversary. That's not for another six weeks yet.'

'No.' Oliver conceded the point.

'And it's not because Tom and Gina are coming tomorrow, is it?'

Oliver grinned. 'Heaven forbid!'

But, surprisingly enough, the two brothers had mended their differences. Tom had had to accept that Grace had never been interested in him, and although he had dated Gina on the rebound, their relationship had lasted much longer than anyone had expected.

Which was why, with Gina's eighteenth birthday only days away, Mr and Mrs Ferreira had invited them to spend a few days with them at the villa. Whether anything serious would come of the relationship, no one knew, but Grace suspected that Gina was more than a match for her thirty-two-year-old boyfriend.

Now, however, she frowned, and taking pity on her, Oliver said, 'It's exactly a year ago today that we made love for the first time.' And as her face cleared and she caught her breath in delight, he added, 'This room and that sofa have very dear memories for me.'

'Oh, Oliver!' Grace wound her arms around his neck. 'That's so romantic!'

Oliver looked a little sheepish then. 'Yeah, well, don't let Tom hear you say that.'

'Why not?' Grace arched her brows teasingly. 'Knowing the way he always tries to copy what you do, would you begrudge Gina a similar experience?'

'In a word, yes,' said Oliver drily, taking her hand and pulling her towards the sofa where he had experienced so much pleasure—and so much grief when she'd sent him away. He drew her down beside him and cupped her face in his hand. 'I love you, Mrs Ferreira. And I wanted to do something to show you how much.'

Grace quivered, but when his hand went to the buttons on her bodice, she caught his fingers in hers. 'You don't intend to—not here?'

'Why not?'

'But Alex—and Maria—'

'Alex had a bottle half an hour ago. And Maria has strict orders not to come downstairs without my permission.'

Grace expelled a shaky breath. 'You've thought of everything, haven't you?'

'I hope so. It hasn't been easy, I can tell you.' He continued to open the buttons as he spoke, and then bending towards her, he captured one swollen nipple between his teeth. 'You only agreed to let Alex have a bottle tonight because my mother asked you to.'

Grace felt the sensual pull of his tongue right down to her toes, and she sank back against the cushions, taking him with her. 'You wouldn't want me not to feed our son, would you?' she teased him as he moved to her other breast. She caught her breath as his teeth nipped her. 'That—that would be mean.'

'But just,' said Oliver roughly, his eyes dark and slumberous with passion. 'Can I help it if I get jealous sometimes?'

'There no need to be jealous,' Grace assured him urgently. 'You know how I feel about you.' Then, with his erection hard against her stomach, 'Oh, Oliver, do you think we dare…?'

'I think so,' he said huskily.

And they did.

BETTY NEELS

DEBBIE MACOMBER

JESSICA STEELE

A classic
Christmas
collection...

Christmas to Remember

On sale 5th November 2004

Available at most branches of WHSmith, Tesco, ASDA, Martins,
Borders, Eason, Sainsbury's and all good paperback bookshops.

M344

A story of passions and betrayals...
and the dangerous obsessions they spawn

PENNY
JORDAN
SILVER